Tales of the West of Ireland

James Berry

Tales of the
West of Ireland

edited with a Foreword by
Gertrude M. Horgan

The Dolmen Press

*Set in Pilgrim type and printed
and published in the Republic of Ireland
at the Dolmen Press,
North Richmond Industrial Estate,
North Richmond Street, Dublin 1*

*First published 1966
Second edition 1969
Third edition 1975*

*Distributed in the U.S.A. and in Canada
by Humanities Press Inc., 171 First Avenue,
Atlantic Highlands, N.J. 07716*

ISBN 0 85105 285 1   *hardback*

ISBN 0 85105 286 X   *paperback*

Contents

Part One : TALES OF MAYO

Part Two: TALES OF CONNEMARA

Foreword

James Berry, the author of these TALES OF THE WEST OF IRELAND, was a farmer by vocation and a narrator of traditional tales by avocation. He was born in Bunowen, near Louisburgh, County Mayo, in 1842, and a number of his early recollections are centred around the persons and events of the Great Famine. His parents were John Berry and Bridget O'Malley. References to the O'Malley clan and to the Western Owls of the O'Malleys predominate in the tales which in his old age he recalled from oral narration for publication in *The Mayo News* for the benefit of posterity in the years 1910-1913.

Berry's education was received in the hedge schools of his native region and was supplemented by the guidance given to his later reading by his uncle, Father Ned O'Malley, Parish Priest of Carna in Connemara. In his youth, James Berry used to visit his uncle, and it was in Carna that he met Sarah Greene, the young Connemara girl who was later to become his wife. After his marriage he settled in Carna where he reared his family, toiled as a farmer to support them, and persevered in his lifelong devotion to the art of storytelling. In 1914 he was buried in Mynish cemetery where he now rests beside the bodies of his wife and his mother.

His daughter, Miss Helena Berry, who still lives in Carna, recalls that her father spent many hours at night by the fire recording the traditional tales in numerous notebooks. She remembers that when he was dying, he called his wife to his side and made her burn a heap of ledgers which contained the stories he was still preparing for publication, saying that he did not wish anyone else to tamper with the narratives.

The folk tales which James Berry recorded and in some cases invented do not possess the range and imaginative quality of William Carleton's writing, but in many ways the Mayo man's delineation of the faith of the peasants and the devotion of their priests reveals aspects of the life of the Irish people which Carleton,

who wrote often for temporal gain and as a paid pro-
pagandist, frequently burlesques and derides. D. J.
O'Donoghue notes that Carleton was prepared to write
for any and every side provided he received payment.
By contrast, James Berry wrote tales out of love for his
people and his country.

In arranging the tales in this volume, I have en-
deavoured to remain true to the art of Irish story-
tradition and to the spirit of James Berry. The editing
process throughout has been controlled by a desire to
modernize the presentation of the material so that a
number of short tales which were previously combined
in lengthy summaries of incidents have been separated
and given their just due. The division of the work into
Tales of Mayo and Tales of Connemara is my desig-
nation, not Berry's, and the titles of a number of the
tales are the responsibility of the editor. All things
considered, this collection of tales is offered 'To James
Berry and the people of Ireland with love !'

G.M.H.

Acknowledgements

While studying Anglo-Irish literature in Ireland in 1964-1965, I spent several months at a cottage owned by Mr. and Mrs. P. J. Kelly of Westport, and located at Old Head, on the shore of Clew Bay, a short distance from Croagh Patrick. Through conversations with the Kellys I became interested in the work of James Berry, their favourite Irish author, a native of Bunowen near Louisburgh in County Mayo. At the time I was engaged in research on the career and accomplishments of William Carleton, the best known teller of Irish tales in the nineteenth century. Carleton's tales were at least available, although no recent editions have been published, with the exception of a small collection edited by Anthony Cronin.

In the case of James Berry, I found that his tales had been published in *The Mayo News*, and since the files of this newspaper for the years in question had been destroyed, the only available copies were those which had been saved by Mayo residents, or were in the files of the periodical collection of the British Museum. A heritage which belongs to the people of Ireland, a number of traditional tales of Mayo and Connemara, was on the verge of being forgotten unless these stories could be collected and edited in permanent form. This was the task to which I dedicated myself in gratitude to my Irish ancestors, the Horgans of County Cork, the Coynes of Athlone, and the O'Neills and Donahues of County Tyrone.

To Mr. and Mrs. P. J. Kelly, their son, Father Vincent Kelly, and their daughter Breta I am indebted for the preservation of a number of the Berry tales, and for their warm-hearted enthusiasm and encouragement. Mr. Seamus Durkan of Louisburgh devoted many hours to accompanying me on drives throughout the area to the townlands mentioned in these tales. He also introduced me to Mr. Austin O'Reilly, the local historian, who knew James Berry, and who is himself a repository of memories and stories which deserve preservation. A visit to Carna in County Galway led to an interview with Miss Helena Berry, daughter of James, who was happy to grant permission for this edition of her father's tales. Father Leo Morahan, a native of Louisburgh, now teaching at St. Mary's College, Galway, and also serving as editor of *An Coinneal*, a magazine published by Kilgeever Parish, Louisburgh, was most helpful in locating some of the missing tales at the British Museum.

Mr. Liam Miller of The Dolmen Press, to whom I was introduced through the kindness of Mr. William O'Neill of Trumera National School, Mountrath, County Laois, evinced interest in publishing TALES OF THE WEST OF IRELAND as part of a series on Ireland's cultural past. He has been helpful in his suggestions and patient in the necessary delays encountered in preparing the manuscript. The administration of Aquinas College, Grand Rapids, Michigan, where I am a member of the faculty in the Department of English Literature, generously granted me the time and assistance required for the compilation of this volume.

Gertrude M. Horgan

Old Head, County Mayo, July-September, 1964.
Dublin, October, 1964 - January, 1965.
Nantasket Beach, Hull, Massachusetts, August, 1965.

I: TALES OF MAYO

A Parliamentary Election during the Famine

About the year 1848, although the famine was raging and denuding the country of its inhabitants by the thousands each day, a Parliamentary election took place in Mayo which roused the peasantry to a great pitch, and was contested on both sides with extraordinary virulence and determination. One of the candidates was G. H. Moore of Moorehall, the nominee of the Brownes of Westport, for Moore was their near kinsman, an untried man at that time, and the electors of West Mayo distrusted him in consequence of having some of the blood of the notorious Brownes in his veins. One of the reasons for their distrust was a terrible tradition perpetuated by the old men of the West who always said that Denis Browne, the tyrant, was nicknamed 'Soap the Rope' because of all the people he got hanged in 1798 as well as before and after that date. It was said that Browne was responsible for having G. H. Moore's grandfather hanged for some crime, and yet the degenerate son of the man who was slaughtered forgot all about this and married either the daughter or the niece of Denis Browne. I don't know whether this terrible story was true or false, but I do know that I have heard it a thousand times from my infancy until I grew to be a man, and the old men who used to be telling the tale knew what they were talking about, for they knew the Moores who owned one townland in the parish of Louisburgh, namely Aillemore, some four miles west of the town. The Moores were not considered kind landlords either, for their tenants scarcely saw any of their faces, but were left to the mercy of the grasping bailiff.

The other candidate in this election marched beneath the banner of the 'Lion of the fold of Judah', the great

John McHale of Tuam, the great, stalwart, militant prelate with the pale face and the massive Roman nose, who could well be called 'Gregory the Great of Ireland'. Oh, it's often and often I when young and thousands with me, went to meet him all the way towards Lecanvey, carrying evergreen branches high above our heads, and when he would draw near our joyous shouts would rend the air and Croagh Patrick would echo with our cries, for to us he seemed like Conn of the hundred battles triumphantly returning from the wars.

If the Archbishop searched all Ireland he couldn't have found a worse candidate than his nominee, Joe Moore McDonnell of Doocastle, a country squire, who had nothing to recommend him save his drinking proclivities, his vile, immoral, immodest anecdotes, and his colossal stature; but the great Archbishop could find no other candidate, and he was determined to oust Moore at any cost in order to show the Government and the landlords what he could do. Some thought it a rash, forlorn hope, but the Archbishop was undismayed for, like the first Napoleon, he had a staff of priests around him, generals in fact, who were the bravest of the brave, foremost among them being Father Michael Conway, Father Luke Ryan, and Father Michael Curley who, although small in stature, was surely the Roman of them all.

The list of voters in my native parish was much reduced, for the small freeholders were swept away in hundreds by the famine and were mouldering in their grave, and those who remained and withstood its ravages were impudent boddagha who always plumped for the Brownes, so the case seemed dark and hopeless in the West. However, the night before the polling day came around, the then Parish Priest of Louisburgh, Father Pat McManus, gathered all the young men of that town and adjacent villages around him and held a consultation. They disguised themselves and became kidnappers, and they went through the whole parish in gangs and lifted everyone of Browne's plumpers off their beds, abducted and carried them to the P.P.'s house where they remained strictly guarded until the news arrived that Joe Moore McDonnell was returned M.P. for Mayo.

The first man they took off his bed was the old pack-man Pat Malley of Shraugh, who at all times worked tooth and nail for the Brownes of Westport. When seized, Pat began lustily calling for his sons who were great fighting men to come and rescue him. 'Joe Malley,' he shouted, 'where are you? Johnny, Affy, Myles, come here at once with your blackthorns!' But they didn't respond to his call for it was his own sons and others who kidnapped him. They carried him through the fields and had to jump across a sluggish stream called the Glesh before they placed him in Father McManus's parlour. All through this journey the old man kept threatening his abductors that 'as sure as there is a Browne, or a Clendinning or a Hildebrand in Westport ye will pay dearly for this!' The kidnappers were inexorable, however, and they secured him under lock and key.

Just then another gang arrived carrying in old Paddy McGirr, Michael McHale and Michael McDonnell, and soon two or three other gangs arrived carrying old Billy na Mallagh of Glankeen, old Wat Malley of Furmoyle, old Johnny Davy Gibbons of Cloonlara, and old Paddy Gibbons of Roonith, the last-named being Lord Sligo's bailiff in the West, and many others of lesser note too numerous to mention. This wasn't a bad night's work for the kidnappers; they surely gave good value for the whiskey they were drinking, and they well deserved it. This business cost the priest some money, for the kid-nappers could drink whiskey with the gusto of red men, and the abducted plumpers could drink punch by the gallon; they could throw it back and it wouldn't affect them any more than if you were throwing it into a limekiln in full blast. When the old plumpers saw how the game was played and saw plenty of punch on the table, they threw in the sponge and became very good-humoured, and then they set to work hammer and tongs at the punch, and as the night wore on old McGirr proposed that the old packman would spin them a yarn to pass the time away.

Pat Malley's Tale of the Faction Fights
of the Galvanaghs and Gromastoons

'Paddy,' said old McGirr, 'tell us about the faction fights
of the Galvanaghs and the Gromastoons, and what was
the origin of those curious names.' Pat Malley, the old
packman, was in the midst of finishing his twelfth
tumbler of punch, so he finished it up with a smack
before he replied with a smile, 'Oh yes, Mr. McGirr, I
shall with pleasure, but in doing so I will have to call
Irish history to aid me, for I must go into detail which
may seem to you to be out of place, but when I have
finished you will plainly see what I have been driving
at all the time, nor can I explain the thing to the satisfaction of the company without doing so.

'When the Anglo-Normans came over to Ireland with
Strongbow, there was a man named De Exter among
them, and as time went on some of his descendants
grasped a large territory around Swinford and Straide in
this country of ours, and they called themselves Jordans.
Later on, Cromwell came along and drove out the
Anglo-Normans, but in many cases Cromwell gave them
a sort of equivalent holding in the wilds of Connacht.
Anyone who reads Prendergast's *Cromwellian Settlement* can see this for himself. The ones that Cromwell
drove out could take their tenants who wished to follow
them into exile. So Cromwell drove out the Jordans of
Rosslavin, or one of them, and he gave that Jordan a
little patch as an equivalent in the Western Owl of the
O'Malleys, namely Old Head, Legan, Balure, Derrylahan, Ruan and Caraclaggin. All these townlands save
Caraclaggin are now wiped off the map of Ireland and
are encompassed by a double stone wall, and they go
by the name of Wilbraham's farm.

'Jordan had to migrate, and he built his humble home
in Legan on the bright, sunny, western slope of the hill
of Old Head, which commanded a fine view of the
valley of the great Achill mountains, Clare Island, and
the wild, western Atlantic, and there his descendants
dwelt for ages. Four of his tenants, most respectable

people, determined to accompany him into exile to
share his joys and his sorrows with him in the land of
the stranger. One family was named McHale, the ancestor of the McHales of Emlagh; another family was
named Durkan, the ancestor of the Durkans of Caraclaggin, some of whom now reside in Askalaun. A third
family was named McNicholas, the ancestors of the
Nicholsons of Bunowen, who, when they reached the
West, dropped the Mc from their name. As time went
on, the children of these migrants intermarried with the
children of the fine old stock who dwelt along the shore
of the western sea, and in a generation or two they
became so amalgamated and merged that they were all
called Galvanaghs or Galanaghs, because their ancestors
came from the barony of Gallan.

'The last family of the amiable Jordans lived some
forty years ago in Ballyhaunis. Until very lately they
owned some eight acres of sterile land and a two storey
house which was fast beginning to decay, in Kelsallagh.
It stood on the brow of the cliff above the wild waves
in the bleakest spot I have seen. There it stood for ages
in its nakedness without a tree or bush to shelter it or
wave their stunted branches in the wind, and when I
passed it by I always compared it in my mind to an
aged peasant whose kith and kin all lay slumbering in
their graves, and whose children had deserted him and
fled in exile across the dark blue sea, while he was left
perishing and lamenting on the wild seashore with none
to console or comfort him. This was the last bower of
the lost paradise of the Jordans, and they clung to it as
if it were a fairy palace standing in the Elysian fields.
It was the very last remnant of their patrimony in the
West and they clung to it with the tenacious grip of an
octopus until the last of them perished and the stock
became extinct.

'The Gromastoons took their name from an unpal-
atable wild potato called gromastoon, and these obscure
people were something like the Plebeians of ancient
Rome. They lived in Falduff, Kilgeever, Moneen and
other villages east and north of Louisburgh. Surely they
were a very heterogeneous race who lived in squalid

poverty and destitution. Most of them were squatters who had no land save conacre, and so they sowed the potato which grew the largest and most numerous tubers, and that was the gromastoon, so the name stuck to them although they surely detested it, and they detested the Galvanaghs whose status was so far above them. It would take only a small spark to explode a fire and set them at the throats of the people they hated.

'When roused, the Gromastoons were a relentless people who would follow up a quarrel even to the very death. Their capital was Moneen, a sort of town of thatched cabins clustered around the spot where a man named Ody Moran lived some forty years ago, and woe to the benighted traveller who had to pass through it, for what the Bowery and Chinatown are to New York, Moneen was to the people of the West. The Gromastoons were so numerous that they could bring six hundred fighting men to the fields of battle, followed always by three hundred of their squaws.

'The cause of the quarrel between the Gromastoons and Galvanaghs arose in this way. Two old men who were brothers-in-law and who had seen better days, opened an Academy in Moneen. They were Galvanaghs; one taught reading and writing, and the other taught arithmetic which was called cyphering in those days. On a certain day one of the venerable professors thrashed a chap named O'Donnell, whose father was nicknamed "the Rebel", a thorough Gromastoon. Next day "the Rebel" came and thrashed the two venerable professors within an inch of their lives, and when he had them well-thrashed and was leaving the Academy he said, "I'd do that to any two Galvanaghs in the parish." Some days after this O'Donnell was on his way from Balower where he lived to Louisburgh, and he had to pass through Bunowen to get there. A Galvanagh came up to him as he was going by, and said, "Are you as good a man today as the day you thrashed the two old schoolmasters, Billy Lavelle and Owen O'Malley?" "I am that, if not even better," said "the Rebel". "Well now, defend yourself," said the Galvanagh, who proceeded to give him a terrible thrashing. Then the two clans took sides and the war began, a real war between twelve hundred men, for each party brought six hundred fighting men to the field. They fought on Sundays and holydays, at fairs and patterns, at wakes and funerals, and for years every man carried his life in his hand, and even the military could not put the fighting down.

'For a number of years Louisburgh and the country west of it was in a state of siege, and all communication was cut off from Westport, for the road ran through the enemy's stronghold of Moneen, Kilgeever and Falduff. There was no other road then, for the new road from Kelsallagh to Louisburgh wasn't built in those days, and woe to the Galvanagh who attempted to break through the lines held by the Gromastoons !

'On Christmas Day in the year 1829 when the people were coming out from the noonday Mass, the news spread that the Gromastoons were marching on the town nine hundred strong, and a panic set in, for half to two-thirds of the Galvanaghs had been to the midnight Mass and returned to their homes, for they never imagined that the Gromastoons would attack them on that blessed day of all days in the year. Then scouts were sent out on horseback and on foot calling in the absent Galvanaghs, and the town was in a panic and uproar.

'The prospect looked gloomy for the unprepared Galvanaghs, but like Leonidas of old who led his band of hardy veterans to meet the hordes of Persia, Billy Nicholson, the veteran leader of the Galvanaghs, led forth his hardy band, determined to meet the hordes of the enemy and cover himself with glory. He took up a strong position at the end of the street where the road sloped down and the wings of his little band were protected by the houses on both sides.

'The motley hordes drew near, led as usual by Peter Ward, a stone mason of Moneen; they hurled themselves against the Galvanaghs and the battle began. The town re-echoed with the shouts of twelve hundred men engaged in mortal strife, the shrieks of women and the rattle of twelve hundred sticks. The Gromastoons began

to fall in hundreds, for now all the absent Galvanaghs
had hastened to the aid of their comrades, and as the
Gromastoons fell their wives drew them down into a
vacant space which soon was piled high with bodies.
Nothing was heard that blessed day but the rattle of
sticks, the shouting of men and the shrieking of women,
and when the shades of night were closing around them
the Celtic death wail arose on the gale and was wafted
through the town for Jimmy Hoban, a Gromastoon, lay
on the street stark dead with scores of women weeping
around him with the weird cries of so many banshees.

'The battle was over, and the Gromastoons retired,
carrying their wounded with them, most of them
maimed and disfigured for life, but the Galvanaghs had
scarcely a scratch. Wasn't this a nice kind of work on
that blessed day? Of course, there was an inquest held
which resulted in the transportation of many for twenty
years to Van Diemensland. What they suffered there
has been described in the street ballads of those days :

> "So now we're safely landed upon the Australian
>   shore,
> Where thousands of those negroes surrounded o'er
>   and o'er;
> They tackled us like horses as you may understand,
> And they yoked us to the plough, my boys,
>   to plough Van Diemensland." '

How Maura-Nee-Ortha
Won the Race at Ballyknock

Pat Malley, the old packman, tossed back a few tumblers
of punch while Michael McHale tried to get his attention. Finally Paddy, his thirst satisfied, smiled and
looked around him. McHale called across the room to
him, 'Paddy, how did you come by that mare of yours,
Maura-nee-Ortha?'

'I came by her quite accidentally,' said Paddy, 'and I will tell you about it. When I gave up being a packman and got married, I rented the townland of Shraugh which was wasteland from Lord Sligo and I built my home there, and became a cattle jobber. One day I was going to the fair of Ballyheame or perhaps it was to Doon-na-Mona I was going, I cannot recall which, but I was mounted on a six year old gray mare that was rather slow.

'When I drew near my destination I met an old man who was leading a young bay mare with a straddle and baskets on her. She began to prance about and she threw off the baskets and the straddle turned under her belly as she lashed about in a great way so that she soon got rid of the straddle. Then I saw that she was the most beautiful bright bay mare I had ever seen. The simple old peasant was in a rage.

' "What's up with you, man?" I said to him. "Arra man, don't you see what is up with me? Amn't I killed entirely with this rip of a brumach? May the curse of Cromwell fall down on the top iv her head," he said.

' "Why did you buy such a wild one?" I said. "Arra, sure didn't I get grief and misfortune when I got this one?" said he. "But I didn't buy her, I reared her myself. Some four years ago I had an old bay mare who in her time was surely a good one. I lived near Moorehall, and the Moores were always famous for having great horses. They had at that time a wonderful thoroughbred sire, and I bribed the groom who at night let the sire serve my mare, and this is the vagabond she brought me."

' "Would you swap with me?" I said. "Ah! God forgive you for humbugging an old man," he said. "I'll take her as she stands," I said. "Well, then, here she is and my blessing," he replied. I dismounted and took the saddle off my gray mare and placed it on Maura-nee-Ortha's back and drove off, followed by the blessing and prayers of the old man.

'Soon after this they started a horse race in Louisburgh; of course there was no racecourse, only the public road, the distance being from Kilgeever to Louisburgh. There were horses there from Aughagower,

Kilmeenan and elsewhere, and off they went, Maura among them. When they were midway between Moneen and Toureen, as Maura was passing swiftly by, the Aughagower man put his foot under the stirrup of Maura's jockey and shot him out of the saddle. The mare halted until the jockey got back in the saddle and before they reached the Bay of Toureen she swept past the lot of them, nor could her jockey pull her up until she reached Bunowen, and when he got her in hand and turned, she danced through the square in such a way that the old men swore in their excitement. "By G — !" they cried, "she's ready to run to the Killary Bay !"

'At that time Lord Sligo had a racecourse in a portion of his demesne called Ballyknock, which was then one of the most popular and best patronized gatherings in the province. All my friends induced me to enter her for the big race there, and I did so. When the day arrived, most of the people of the West went there to see what Maura could do, and to my horror as the time drew near for starting, my son, Joe Malley, who was to ride her, was blind drunk. I began scolding him, and a vast crowd gathered around us. A man forced his way through the crowd and said, "Paddy, take it easy, I'll ride Maura-nee-Ortha for you." Well, I looked at him then and I saw that he wore a caubeen with a green band around it. The colour and make of his clothes I couldn't tell, for he was enveloped in a dark green coat with a short back, but with skirts reaching the ground. Surely I was astonished at his cheek and was almost tempted to assault him, but yet I held my hand, for I well knew I had no other jockey, and the bell was clanging for the jockeys to be weighed.

' "Very well," I said, "throw off your overcoat." "Not I," he said, "these are my colours when I ride on the Curragh of Kildare." The weighmaster ordered him to throw off his coat. "Oh no," he said, "this is my livery, and you dare not object provided I am the proper weight," said he, and he was the proper weight to the peel of an onion. Then he mounted Maura-nee-Ortha amidst the laughter of the crowd, and the next thing I heard was a shout, "They're off !" There was a field of fourteen horses.

'When he had run about a furlong, my man pulled up Maura and galloped towards me and shouted, "Get a jack-knife and cut off these skirts !" Many knives were pulled out by the crowd and the great skirts fell off in a jiffy and he flew off. He soon returned though, and then I knew I was ruined for life, for I had a good bit of money staked on the mare, as had hundreds from my parish. "Here !" he shouted, "sew on the skirts again. I'm no use without them." How they were sewed on I don't know, for I was dazed, but they were sewed on; he flew off like the wind, followed by the laughter and execrations of the vast audience.

'There was an oblong hillock in the end of the field around which the course wound on the other side, and when the horses were just turning around the bend Maura-nee-Ortha rushed in among them. Then we lost sight of them for a minute or two, a time which seemed like an hour because of the silence and the tension and then a horse came around the bend at the other end of the hillock and the hills reverberated with the shout that went up from the vast crowd as they shouted, "Maura-nee-Ortha is first ! She's coming with the speed of the wind !" Their wild huzzas rent the air, and sure enough it was she, and the people of the West who were there in hundreds shouted again and again, "Hurrah ! Hurrah for Maura-nee-Ortha, the glory and pride of the West !"

'On she came, her brave rider bending towards her ears, for there was a strong wind blowing against them and he knew well how not to retard her speed, and the tail of his great coat floated far behind him like the tail of a meteor rushing through space, and soon she rushed in past the winning post, and those who mocked them at the start were the most vociferous in their praise. There were two furlongs between her and the next horse, another bright bay mare, the property of Colonel Vandalure from the County of Clare. Then the man with the great coat dismounted and vanished, and from that day to this night I have never seen the man with

the great coat who rode Maura-nee-Ortha that day to
victory at Ballyknock.'

'A Cake' in West Mayo

Down to the year of the great famine of 1846 a certain
kind of social gathering in West Mayo was called 'A
Cake'. Such events were of frequent occurrence throughout the various villages, and in a way they resembled
patterns. They were something like the present-day
raffles held to assist some worthy, struggling family,
and were conducted with much decorum and politeness.
Nor was there ever a row or a quarrel at such
gatherings.

Supposing a poor family lost their only cow and had
no earthly means of replacing her. The mother of the
family went to some friendly publican and got from
him on credit five or ten gallons of whiskey, some wine
and cordials. She then went to a baker who baked her
a great, ornamental cake about two or three stone in
weight. Next she engaged the services of a musician;
this was easily done, for the pipes in those days were
as plentiful as blackberries in Autumn. The news was
then spread abroad that 'A Cake' would be held in a
certain village on the next Sunday or holy day.

All the people of the surrounding villages would
gather there in hundreds, decked out in their best
holiday attire. All the marriageable peasant girls appeared in cashmere shawls and fine lace dress caps,
garnished with nosegays and decorated with many
ribbons of various shades and colours. There they would
sit demurely and bashfully with the eyes of their ever-
watchful mothers intent upon them. Vigilant as the
mothers were, the bashful, blushing maidens sent many
a wireless telegraphic message from their dark eyes to

their favourite swains who sat in some distant corner.

The very last gathering of this kind was held in my
native village on the Saint Patrick's day before the
famine, and although I was then only about six years
old, I have a clear and vivid recollection of it, for it
was held quite near the cabin in which I was born.
When I came on the scene all the people were gathered
in a vast crowd, and the piper, a young man, sat on a
chair in the open air playing 'Haste to the Wedding'.
He was six feet four inches in height and admirably
well-shaped, and was surely the most distinguished man
I have ever seen, although he was blind.

This was Martin Moran, the son of a well-to-do
farmer in the locality, considered to be the best player
in Connacht in his day. It was a wonderful and glorious
sight to see him seated and playing, sometimes sweeping
the keys of his pipes with great, long fingers. In after
years when I had grown up, this masterful sweeping of
his pipes filled my mind with visions of Carolan and
the great and grand old harpers of ancient Erin. Martin
became a great favourite of John McHale, the lion of
Tuam, who presented him with a set of pipes which
cost thirty-five pounds, and in presenting them the
Archbishop christened Martin 'the last of the Minstrels'.

In front of the house there was a little sloping lawn
in the centre of which stood a churndash, its handle
driven firmly into the ground. On the upturned boss of
the churndash was spread a white, home-made linen
towel, on which was laid the great ornamental cake.
The custom was that whoever carried in the cake should
call for a round of drinks for the whole gathering. A
young blacksmith of the town who was also a young
man of property, one William Jordan, took in the cake
and called for two gallons of punch, and wine and
cordials for the ladies. Then the spree began in real
earnest, and when it was over the woman was able to
pay her creditors and to clear the price of a little cow
as well, for cows were quite cheap in those days.

Among all the vast assembly at 'the Cake' I noticed
three old men who sat by themselves, and who in
appearance and dress differed as much from those

around them as the sun differs from the moon. These three noble-looking old men belonged to the eighteenth century and lived far into the nineteenth. They were the last of their generation I have seen, and their garb was of the best material that money could buy; in fact, it was the garb of Henry Grattan, for the rich peasantry of their day affected the garb of the Upper Ten.

These three men were dressed alike; each of them held a fine top silk hat in his hand, and their hair which was cropped somewhat short grew luxuriantly on the crown of their heads, although I am sure they seldom combed it. Their high shirt-collars were of smooth home-made linen, and their cravats were black silk handkerchiefs brought twice around the neck and knotted carefully and neatly in front. Each wore a double-breasted, bottle-green broadcloth coat and a double-breasted vest of the same material. They wore tight-fitting knee-breeches, and their legs were encased in brownish, olive-coloured box cloth, buttoned up to the knee leggings. Each of these clean-shaven men carried a polished, well-kept blackthorn stick with a gimlet hole near where they held it, through which was inserted a leather whang, both ends knotted together.

These three old men belonged to the faction-fighting days. When going into action they inserted the hand into the whang and pulled it up on the wrist. This was a wise precaution, for if they were struck on the hand by an antagonist, although they had to drop the stick, it still hung on the arm and they soon recovered it and returned to the fray. Some of the faction fighters went into battle armed with two sticks, one of which they used as a shield or buckler, while they assailed and struck with the other. They fought for glory, and sometimes for pleasure. They did not fight in order to kill; they did not use jack knives, stones or bars of iron like the other men of those times, for they were as honourable as Sarsfield, and as brave as Myles the Slasher.

One of these grand old men was a Mr. John David Gibbons of Cloonlara, whose ancestors were the feudal kings of Glankeen. There he sat, stately even in his old age, with his distinctive, hereditary Roman nose, the hall-mark of the fine old clan to which he belonged. Next to him was a Mr. Walter James O'Malley of Furmoyle, who claimed to be descended not from Grainne, but from Doodarra O'Malley of the long ships, who lost his life while attempting to pillage the inhabitants of the dark blue Isles of Aran. The last man of this triumvirate was a Mr. O'Malley of Shraugh, who claimed to be descended from Mlaghlan fodda an rapier, that is, Malachie of the broad sword, who slew many of the Brownes of Westport who thought to seize his property. Spurred on by the desire for revenge, the first Lord Altamount offered his sister in marriage to any man who would fight and kill Mlaghlan in single combat. An English gentleman named Cox, who was considered the best swordsman in Europe, came over from London and challenged Mlaghlan. Tradition states that this Mr. Cox had a wooden leg.

On the day after his arrival, Cox drove out to Belclare with the Brownes, and on the road they met a man. 'Who is that wonderful looking man whose hands reach below the knees and who carries his great sword in his left hand to keep it from clanging against the ground, and who is surely left-handed?' asked Cox. 'That is the man you have challenged and will fight tomorrow,' said Miss Browne, his prospective wife, and Cox seemed to tremble.

Next day they met in a historic field, the fatal field of Annagh where the pagan king of Killadangan and his worthless servant Thulera lie buried. With them sleep the twin sons of William O'Malley who fought here and ran each other through the body on account of a lady. On this day there was another grave to be filled on this field. Mlaghlan fodda an rapier and his clan were the first to arrive, and the Brownes, Cox and their plundering followers came soon after. The combatants threw off their upper garments and rolled up their shirt sleeves. There they stood beneath the shadow of Croagh Patrick, the Saxon and the Celt confronting each other. A clash of steel sounded in the terrible silence; then there came another clash of steel and yet another followed by a groan, for Mlaghlan had driven his terrible claymore to the hilt through the heart of the Saxon, and all was over. So Cox lies sleeping beside the Irish chieftains, wooden leg and all. Mlaghlan and his clan attacked the Brownes who fled the field, nor did they look behind them until they reached their stronghold which crowned the summit of Curranalurgan.

At 'the Cake' there was present another man, a simpleton from birth, who always wore the cast-off clothes of a policeman. He belonged to the far West, but he made the town of Louisburgh his happy hunting ground. He was called Maurteen Omadaun, but he judged and settled a lawsuit which the County Court judge, the Judge of Assizes, and the parish priest had been unable to decide. This case was similar to the one in scripture, the one Solomon decided so wisely. The particulars are worth recording.

Until the famine time the small farmers along the sea coast sent their horses to summer grazing on the great hills which surround Doolough. These mountains are very precipitous, and on hot days the horses would stand on the brow of the cliff in order to inhale the cool breeze from the lake and to escape the stinging wasps. Then the eagles, with which these cliffs abounded, would swoop down upon them, dashing against their heads and striking the horses in the eyes with their strong pinions in order to make them restive and fall headlong to the dark glens below where the eagles could gorge themselves on their flesh.

In a certain village there were two men, each of whom had a mare with a filly foal at foot, and the two foals were alike in colour so that it was impossible to know one from the other. These two men sent the mares to graze on Mucelrea, the most precipitous of all the mountains. Like all the rest of the horses, the mares and their foals stood on the brow of a cliff and the eagles swooped down and drove one of the foals over the cliff to be dashed to pieces before it reached the bottom. Then the remaining foal began suckling both of the mares and continued to do so until the owners came for the horses; the question was to which mare did the foal belong, since she was suckling on both. There was much scolding and unpleasantness, and then the men went to law. When it reached the barrister at the Quarter Sessions he could not decide the case. When it reached the Judge of Assizes, he was unable to decide, so he turned the matter over to the Parish Priest to arbitrate. His Reverence gave it mental thought and reflection, but he found that he was unable to solve the problem assigned to him and he was in a quandary, for he said that no man on earth could decide it.

One evening he was seated on a chair at the door of his neat, thatched cottage with a black velvet skullcap on his head, for he was aged and quite bald, when he saw Maurteen Omadaun go by. 'Come here,' he said, and the simpleton came to him. 'Arra Martin avic,' said the saintly old man, 'did you hear that the case about the foal is left to my settlement?' 'I did,' said Martin. 'Well then,' said he, 'it will fail me.' 'It is the simplest case on earth,' replied the fool. 'I would settle that case in five seconds.' 'Arra, Martin Grady, do you tell me so?' said the priest. 'I do,' said he. 'Well then, Martin,' said His Reverence, 'I place the case in your hands.' 'Very well,' answered the simpleton. 'Send word to the men to take the mares and the foal into town tomorrow.' 'I will,' said the priest.

The news spread that Maurteen was to arbitrate and deliver judgment the next morning on this peculiar, complicated case, so a great gathering took place of the townsmen and the people from the adjacent villages. In those days a great barrier or weir spanned the Louis-burgh river some distance above the bridge; this weir backed up the stream and turned it into a large pond or reservoir whose northern shore was a level, sandy strand. This pool was called poolgorrive. 'Take down the mares and the foal to the poolgorrive,' ordered Maurteen. The people wondered at this command, but still they obeyed the mandate of the arbitrator and judge. 'Now,' said Maurteen, 'place the mares on the strand with their heads to the water,' and it was done. 'Carry out the foal to the middle of the weir and cast

him into the pond.' Several men threw the foal into the
pond.

When the foal came to the surface it began to neigh,
and immediately one of the mares plunged into the
water and swam towards the foal which she caught by
the back of the neck and pulled ashore while the other
mare took no interest in the proceedings. 'The mare
who saved the foal is its mother, for Nature has asserted
itself,' declared Maurteen, and the owners and all the
people agreed with him, and they also asserted that
Maurteen Omadaun had placed Solomon somewhat in
the shade. Then they took him on their shoulders and
carried him in triumph through the town.

This simple creature who proved to be so wise was
supported all during his life by a wealthy matron of the
town. Her husband owned a corn mill, and when the
famine set in the mill was grinding corn day and night
for the farmers who held their ground against the ravages of the blight. The farmers paid the owner in meal
in lieu of cash. The stones or quarters of meal were
turned to good account by the miller's grand old wife,
for she got women to boil it into stirabout, and for
three long and weary years she fed hundreds of starving
people by day and night, and during all that time she
saved many hundreds from death by hunger. May the
shamrocks forever bloom and entwine above her grave,
and the brightest sunbeams shine upon it. She often
entertained Dives at her table, but she gloried in always
having Lazarus as her honoured guest. Such was old
Mrs. Paddy McGirr of blessed memory.

The three old men at 'the Cake' seemed to take no
interest whatever in the dancing and hilarity which surrounded them, for they were engrossed in a discussion of
the old times. 'Pat,' said Walter O'Malley to the last of
the packmen, 'do you remember the Sunday we went to
church, the Sunday the priest lent his flock to the parson
in the year 1800?' 'Indeed, I was one of them,' said the
packman. 'I never heard about that,' said Mr. Gibbons
in great astonishment. 'I will tell you all about it,'
said Pat.

'When the Protestant Church was built in Louisburgh,

the first parson sent to occupy it was an Englishman
named Vernon, a son of one of the oldest families in
England, the Vernons of Hadden Hall. He fell in love
with an actress and married her, so his friends disowned
him and cast him off. When he arrived in Louisburgh,
the Parish Priest, Father William Ward, became his
inseparable friend, and each alternate day they dined
with each other, and they took long walks, linked arm
in arm. The poor young man, who once was senior
wrangler in Cambridge University, had only three
Protestants, one of whom was the sexton, in his congregation. Vernon wasn't long in town when the sexton,
a married man, seduced the parson's wife and they
decamped, leaving the parson covered by shame and
humiliation. The priest pitied his forlorn condition.

'One day when returning from a long walk with the
priest, the parson said, "This is, I fear, our last walk,
Father Ward." "Why?" asked the priest. "Because my
Bishop, that is Dr. Beresford, Bishop of Tuam, will be
here on Sunday, and when he sees I have no flock he
will close the church, and on next Monday I will be a
homeless man and a wanderer." "Indeed you won't,"
said the priest, "for I won't have it." "How can you
prevent it?" said the parson. "Oh, quite easily," replied
Father Ward, "for on next Sunday I will lend you my
congregation. On that day when Mass is over I'll send
my flock down to church to you, and believe me, old
Beresford will be both charmed and astonished at
beholding all your converts. Will that save you?" "Oh,
certainly it will," said the parson.

'On Sunday when Mass was over, the priest took the
congregation into his confidence and addressed them in
their own simple manner of speaking, for there is no
better way of arousing the sympathy of the Celt than
to urge them to action in the dialect to which they are
accustomed. "Arra musha let ye all walk down to the
crathereen and fill the church for him and sorra bit of
harm it will ever do ye," said His Reverence. "The poor
forlorn Kegriagh, let ye save him out of danger. It
wasn't enough trouble for the deerough, his rip of a
wife, to make off with old Hawkshaw, but now they

will take the bit and sup out of the crathereen's mouth. Oh, wirra wirra go dea sho go dea schoch." The whole congregation was moved to tears, and left the chapel and sailed down to the Protestant Church and filled it to capacity. The old bishop was charmed and declared they were the finest congregation he ever saw, and he dismissed them after giving his benediction. Ever afterwards the people prided themselves on the work of that Sunday, and they laughed and boasted at how they had fooled old Bishop Beresford, the Protestant Bishop of Tuam.'

The Three Druidical Swords of Casey

Midway between Old Head and the Killary, along the southern shore of Clew Bay, lies Lough Casey, convenient to the little village of Emlagh. It is an interesting sheet of water encompassed on all sides by monotonous scenery, but this insignificant lake has an interesting traditional history which is unique in the annals of Ireland. On the sandy shores of the lake there stood in a group firmly embedded in the sand three tall lintels or flags about five feet high; these were called by the peasantry of the West the Clavie Chaosagh, or the Swords of Casey. There they had stood since the days of the Firbolgs and the De Dananns, the menace and the terror of all the people who dwelt West of the Reek since the earliest ages and down almost to our day. There they stood, the Druidic Swords which since the days of the pagan ancestors slew some thousands of people; the terrific flags which immolated the powerful tyrants, the scandal-givers and the seducers. How on earth could these harmless looking flags slay or wound any man or woman? Here is how they did it, according to tradition.

Suppose a poor person was robbed and plundered by a tyrant, or suppose that an honest person was wrongfully accused of theft, or a virtuous female wrongfully

accused of unchastity, there was no tribunal in the old
or penal times to which they could appeal for justice
and thereby vindicate their characters and reputations.
Were they then to bear all this ignominy lying down,
these peasants with their Celtic temperaments? Surely
it would be hard to expect them to do this, and indeed
they did not meekly submit to these injustices. As a
last resort they appealed to the Swords of Casey, and,
believe me, they got satisfaction, for the swords killed
the tyrant or the traducer.

How was this done? First, the person who had been
wronged fasted three days and nights and then went out
to the swords and performed some kind of station
around them, going the wrong way, and uttering some
horrid incantation according to the liturgy of the
Druids. Then this person knelt and upset the sand at the
foot of the swords; immediately a tremendous cyclone
swept the country, causing much damage to the peasantry, and at the same time the person who was responsible for the injustice of a diabolical accusation or deed
against another fell dead, no matter where he or she
chanced to be at the time.

About the year 1800 there lived in a certain village in
the West a bailiff nicknamed the Plothy, and like all
bailiffs we have ever seen, he was a heartless villain. In
the same village with him there lived a young married
couple just beginning the world, as they say, but it
pleased God to call away the husband who died of a
colic, leaving a widow and three children to weep. The
bailiff swooped down and seized the dead man's little
substance, leaving the young widow and her babies quite
destitute, for he even took away their food. The woman
became demented as she saw her children perishing of
hunger, so she determined to appeal to the Swords of
Casey. She fasted seventy-two hours and then she set
out for the swords which were seven miles distant.
She performed the curious station, concluding it by
kneeling down and upsetting the sand. A cyclone swept
through the country, and at that very moment the
bailiff who was talking to a mason whom he had building a house, fell over on the scaffold. He began kicking

and frothing as if in an epileptic seizure, and he expired
shortly after being carried into his house.

This is the last case recorded in tradition, and it
caused such a sensation that it reached the ears of the
then Archbishop of Tuam, Dr. Skerrett, who determined
to have a trial with the druidic swords. There was no
Louisburgh in those days, for the ground on which it
now stands was then all overgrown with white and
black thorn and strewn with granite boulders. Since
time immemorial it was in the Arcadian village of
Aillemore that Confirmation was administered; consequently, there must have been some sort of a church
there. In those days it must have been a very public
place, although now it is one of the most unfrequented
villages of the West.

When the summer winds began to blow, the Archbishop arrived in Aillemore. He hastened down to Lough
Casey and assisted by his priests he dug up the swords.
He then placed them in a boat and cast them into the
middle of the lake, after which he returned in a jubilant
mood to Aillemore. When he awoke the next morning,
the first news he heard was that the Swords of Casey
were standing firmly in their original position on the
shore of the lake. The Archbishop put on his full
pontificals, took his Crozier in his hand and marched
down once more to Lough Casey. When he beheld the
terrible pillar stones standing in the same spot he became enraged and ran towards them, smiting them with
his Crozier until they fell. Then he took a sledge and
smashed them into fragments, and taking the fragments
into a boat, he rowed out to sea and cast them into the
ocean where they sank beneath the dark waves and
were never again seen on the shores of Lough Casey.

The Tragic Love of Jimmy McDonough

Should you chance to wander through Bunowen, a village on the southern shore of Clew Bay in West Mayo, the road which runs through it when it nears the sea branches off in two directions. One fork leads to the north and passes a neat, thatched cottage well sheltered by trees in which there lived some fifty years ago an amiable peasant named McEvilly. The other road runs towards the north-west by the door of a cottage surrounded by hawthorn trees, in which there lived a man named Berry, who was equally amiable. The reason why I have mentioned the names of men who now lie mouldering in their graves is in order to locate clearly where the hero of my story was born and raised.

Between these two roads, just where they branched off, a green, wedge-shaped little lawn sloped down to the crossroad, and on the little table-land at the head of this slope there stood for many generations a well-kept country house. It had an eastern aspect and commanded a fine view of Croagh Patrick and the great range of dark blue mountains which stretched away southwards to Killary Bay. In this house there lived in 1848 a family named McDonough consisting of nine children who were orphans, for both their parents died of famine fever in 1847, not through want or destitution, for they left a considerable sum of what the peasantry call dry money, and other means besides. There were six boys and three girls, almost all full-grown except two little chaps who were my juvenile comrades. They were all fair-haired, fair-skinned and freckled, and they were considered the best looking family in the half parish in which they lived. Their names were Jimmy, Owen, Pat, John, Affey, Martin, Ellen, Mary and Peggy.

Jimmy was a great favourite with the people and considered to be the finest young man West of the Reek. The colour of his hair was hard to define; it seemed to be either a light nut-brown or a delicate auburn shade, and it was short and curly to the top of his head. He had the sweetest and most sonorous voice of any mortal. I do believe he could read and write, and was great at figures. He was wonderfully well-shaped, as fleet as a wild deer, and he stood well over six feet. When he was called on to sing at the then frequent social gatherings, there would be a stampede towards the chamber where Jimmy was entertaining.

Just a mile from his home stood the little village of Toureen where there lived a poor peasant named Anthony Shiffell who had a full-grown family, one of them being a girl of twenty-two who was surely the most beautiful girl I have ever seen. Her father had no fortune to give her, but still she had great expectations, for it was well-known that certain relatives would give her a dowry of many thousands of pounds provided she got a rich man for a husband. Consequently, her parents and relations watched and guarded her every movement with the sleepless vigilance of Cerberus for fear she should choose her own partner for life. And yet somehow Maggie Shiffell fell desperately in love with Jimmy McDonough and he with her. It was the old, old story, and a silent war began to prevent a wedding.

The parents and relations who twigged it, as if by intuition, tried all sorts of stratagems to out-manoeuvre them, for although Maggie and Jimmy met once a week in the Shiffell home, Maggie was strictly guarded, and it took three long, weary years before the pair had the chance of meeting secretly. Of course, during these years the lovers did a fair share of telegraphy with the eyes and communicated their feelings in a hundred and one little ways well-known to youths and maidens. Wise men inform us that those who wait patiently find what they wait for, and it came true in this instance.

On a certain Sunday in the glorious month of June, all the Shiffells went to a wedding, leaving Maggie to mind the house, moroya, but that was not their motive; they were afraid that she would elope with some boy who would be at the wedding. In the evening, Jimmy was on his way home from the house of a shoemaker who lived in the village of Moneen, and as he was passing Shiffell's door he heard Maggie calling him.

'Conla of the golden locks, come in, I want you,' she cried, and his heart gave a jump.

She was seated at the window holding a book in her hand with her index finger between its leaves. He took it out of her hand and he saw that it was a great book she was reading, *The Imitation of Christ*. The peasant girls of those days never saw a magazine, a journal, a novel, or a penny novelette; consequently they became the best wives and mothers to be met on earth.

Maggie stood up to face him, and surely she was grand to look at. She was of medium height, and had nut-brown hair tinged with copper above the ears towards the temples from which the curls rose above her full and ample brow. Her eyes were dark blue, and her complexion was like a rose leaf. She wore a dark brown cashmere dress with a tight-fitting bodice, and around her wonderfully white neck there stood a ruffle of white lace. This noble-minded girl was as wise as she was fair. 'Now, Jimmy,' she said, 'we have got the chance we have long wished for; let us make good use of it, for it's our first and last chance. Let there be no frivolity between us. Let us understand each other now, once and for all, and proceed to arrange matters for the future. Believe me, we need to be quick, for the dark clouds are beginning to hover over me. Let us declare our feelings towards each other. Do you love me honestly and dearly?' 'Oh, God knows that, and you ought to know it too,' he answered fervently. 'I do,' she said, 'but I wanted to hear it from your lips, and now listen to me. As great as your love is for me, my love for you is ten times greater. Be always ready, for if hard pressed I will fly to you, and then we will walk into the chapel and get married, and then we'll sail away to the land of the setting sun, and God will do the rest. And should we fail in a struggle for existence, and should I languish and pine away and die, my spirit will hover over you, and when you die I will meet you on the white strand of the world beyond. Then I will embrace and kiss you and we'll wander hand in hand together for evermore through the ever-green flowery meadows, the shady bowers, and the palm groves in the bright land of the blest.'

She twined her hands around his neck, drew down
his head and looked into his dark hazel eyes, and kissed
him. 'Now,' she said, 'our contract is sealed. That is the
first kiss I have ever given to mortal man, and it shall
be the last until you kiss me at the altar rail when I
am your wedded bride.' Then they parted, but they
never saw each other again in this life.

Jimmy went home with his head in the air, the happiest man in Ireland. Some three weeks afterwards the
McDonough children were having tea in their well-kept
little parlour when two of Jimmy's comrades came in
and sat down. They were smiling and giggling. Jimmy
was never afraid by night or day of either the living or
the dead, but when he saw false friends smirking, a
terrible fear caught hold of him. All his nerves became
unstrung. 'Any news, boys?' said Ellen McDonough to
the pair of visitors. She was the oldest of the family
and acted as mother to the orphaned children. 'Did ye
not hear it?' they asked. 'No, what is it?' she replied.
'That Maggie Shiffell got married this morning to some
man from a distant parish,' said one. 'What is he like?'
asked Ellen. 'He is a large brute aged about fifty, and
it's said he is pockmarked. They've gone off to his
home,' said the other.

Jimmy had the cup raised to his lips, and his hand
began to shake as if he were stricken with palsy. His
great fingers failed to hold the cup which fell on the
saucer with a crash, shattering both pieces. This drew
the attention of all the company towards him. There
he sat, shaking violently from head to foot, and with
his teeth chattering. 'Oh, Jimmy dear, what ails you?'
asked Ellen, but never a word did she get in reply. The
false friends left hurriedly, for they saw they had
almost killed him.

When night set in and the children were fast asleep in
their beds, Jimmy arose and dressed himself in his
Sunday clothes. He lit a rush lamp and placed it in the
claw of the rude iron candlestick. Next he filled his
powder flask and filled his shotgun and placed it in
position across his shoulders. On tiptoe he went to each

bed and silently kissed his brothers and sisters. He opened the door and quickly latched it behind him, and he fled without a farthing in his pockets from all those he loved so dearly, his friends and relations, and the old ancestral home.

Next morning at dawn Ellen was awakened by hearing her two youngest brothers with whom Jimmy slept, calling out, 'Where is Jimmy?' She sprang out of bed, but Jimmy of the golden curls and the wonderful voice was nowhere to be found, and the Celtic tale of the orphan children's wailing was wafted through the village. The villagers came running and gathered around them, but their sympathy availed little, for Jimmy, their glory and pride, had fled forever. The two old men whom I mentioned at the beginning of this story, McEvilly and Berry, saddled their horses and went in search of him, for what Mat Donovan was to the people of Knocknagow, Jimmy McDonough was to the people of Bunowen. Alas, they never found him, although they inquired all along the road to Castlebar where they went thinking that he might have gone there and enlisted. Some time afterwards a man wrote from England stating that he saw Jimmy in a Dragoon regiment, but this tale turned out to be untrue. Another neighbour named Devany wrote home saying that he saw him in Philadelphia, and this aroused the McDonough children who determined to emigrate.

Ellen and Mary began baking much oatmeal bread and laying up a stock of butter for the voyage, for the company who owned the 'coffin ships' did not give the emigrants one-fifth of the food supply needed for the voyage. When all was ready, the children cast open the doors of their ancestral home and left it derelict. They abandoned the farm they had made productive and fertile by the sweat of their brows, and others of the village did the same so that the landscape was disfigured with the derelict, ruined homes of the peasantry, and their deserted farms lay fallow. Nor had the peasantry who remained the courage to occupy them, for as a result of all they had seen and gone through during the time of the famine, they thought the end of the world was at hand.

The McDonough children and many more of the peasantry of the West went on board a brig named the 'William Barrington' in Inishlyre and sailed down Clew Bay. The peasantry gathered in hundreds to bid a last farewell to the relations and friends they would never again see on earth. They mounted the hill of Old Head, some of them carrying huge bundles of straw which they would light on the cliffs as the brig bore down on the wild headland. When the ship drew near, they lit some of the straw and began shouting. Some of the females shrieked and gesticulated wildly, and as the brig was passing they ran along the tremendous cliffs to light more straw on the brow of the cliff of Derrylahan. Then they rushed westward and set more straw blazing on the summit of Fairy Hill. Next they crossed the Bunowen river, ran along the strand and climbed the hill of Carramore. As the brig passed quite near this hill they began shouting, calling their relatives by name, and setting ablaze the last bundles of straw. Wailing and weeping, they threw themselves on the ground and watched the brig until she disappeared below the western horizon; then many of the females swooned and had to be carried home.

I was just eight years old at the time, and took part in the demonstration of grief on Fairy Hill as the McDonough children sailed away. A giant nicknamed Tommy Paddagh swung me on his back and ran madly into the crowd, crossed the river and along the strand of Carramore, and then climbed the steep hill and placed me on its summit. I shall forever remember that terrible scene. Ah, it's many and many a steep hill and high mountain I have climbed since then, but the memory of that night of grief and mourning on the hill of Carramore is deeply embedded in my heart.

Later we learned the details of the voyage of the brig 'William Barrington' to America. When the coffin-ship reached mid-ocean the emigrants began to die, for the hold in which they were confined had no ventilation and became as hot as an oven, turning into a death hold. The youngest of the McDonough orphans, Affey and

Martin, were among the first to die and be buried at sea; this slaughter of the innocents continued until they almost reached the land. After a journey of nineteen long and weary weeks, the brig reached America where she vomited out from the hold the emaciated, half-starved white slaves, or all that remained of them, into the city of Philadelphia. From that day until the last of the family died, the McDonough children never again saw their darling Jimmy of the golden hair.

And what was Jimmy's beloved Maggie doing all during this time? When the giant took her to his enchanted castle, she was morbid. She sat down in her room, her hands in her lap, and there she sat staring at nothing, apparently. She was looking inward at her lost love with the eyes of her mind, however, and for eleven months she continued in that position, for she had lost all interest in life. At the end of that period the pangs of child labour set in, but she had no strength to bring forth the baby, nor did she realize her condition. She never called for help, so she died where she knelt beside her bed, and the great marriage match that had been made for her ended in dust and ashes. How this phenomenal marriage was brought about, no person could or did find out; surely some supernatural power had been at work to overthrow her love and destroy her life. Those who were the human agents who caused her death and turned the McDonough orphans into exiles and sent two of them to the bottom of the wild Atlantic, will surely have a bad half hour when they stand before the judgment seat of God.

Jimmy McDonough's Flight to Connemara

When Jimmy McDonough fled from his home and kindred, he determined to reach some country where he could hide himself and never be traced, and he knew where that country lay. Just beside the house in which he was born and near the cabin in which I first saw the

light of day, there dwelt an old peasant with thin,
aquiline features, a man who was blind in one eye and
who had a great blue scar on his high, full, narrow
brow, for he was an old rebel who fought at the battle
of Castlebar and received these two wounds at the
battle of Ballinamuck. When I used to look at him and
whenever memory brings him before my mental vision,
I used to then and ever since think of Hannibal.

The old man's name was Jimmy Malley, but he was
always called by the nickname 'Go-go' which he won
in his escape from Ballinamuck. He remained in Southern Connemara, which was then the wildest portion of
Ireland, for twenty-five years, supporting himself as a
quack doctor, for in those days the medicine man was
in high repute among the wild, simple natives. When he
was quite an aged man, he returned to his native village
of Bunowen and was astonished to find his wife still
living and his family, consisting of three daughters and
a son, fully grown and in comparative comfort. They
received the old, veteran patriot with open arms, nor
was he in his old age ever afterwards heeded by the
Government.

This old man's house after his return from exile, when
I was a child, was during the winter nights the favourite
rendezvous of all the youths and maidens of the village,
as well as of the wee chaps, for Jimmy was forever re-
counting his adventures and dangers both in field and
flood, and we small chaps used to pray fervently that he
would never cease these tales. He was forever describing
the wild land of his exile, its almost interminable moors
and swamps, the thousands of lakes, sluggish mountain
streams and roaring torrents of a land without roads,
paths or trails, a rough granite-strewn region which
abounded in caves, a land where the king's writ never
ran, and where never a word of English was uttered.
When the refugee reached this region he was received
with open arms by the primitive natives who were as
true as steel, and he was as safe as if he had taken refuge
in the moon.

The natives were as primitive in their manners and
customs as our ancestors were a thousand years ago.

They had many faults, but most of their faults and failings leaned to virtue's side. The males from earliest boyhood, like our pagan ancestors, delighted in athletic sports, especially hurling and wrestling, which their descendants still continue to engage in every Sunday of the year on the sandy beaches along the seashore. When these lads become full-grown they excel as wrestlers. About eight years ago, a young man named Pat Connolly from the vicinity of Carna in Connemara, went off to Scotland, carrying with him his fame as a wrestler. When he reached Glasgow he was picked up by a Sporting Club which took him on a tour through the principal cities of the British Isles, and no man he met ever threw him on the mat. For the past two years he has journeyed through the United States and Canada, and he has never met there a man fit to throw him, so he now claims to be the world's champion wrestler. He is a splendid young man, a native of Connemara, and surely a credit to his land.

When Jimmy McDonough closed the door of his ancestral home behind him and fled from Bunowen, he determined to reach Southern Connemara, the region where old Malley had found refuge, and hide there forever. He placed his gun on his arm and set his face to the South, nor did he ever look around him until he reached Doolough. He sat down in a little glen beside that terrible spot in the goat track which overhangs the dark lake called the Stroppabue. The little glen slanted down to the cliff, and was thickly overgrown with tall, wide-leaved, wild fern which grew luxuriantly above the graves of his much-wronged, famished countrymen who had perished in this desolate pass some three years before, a dreadful tragedy which might well be called the slaughter of the innocents.

Death at Doo Lough

In the spring of 1847, some six hundred of the starving
peasantry of the West thronged into the town of Louisburgh, seeking food or a ticket for admission to the
workhouse from the Relieving Officer. He informed
them that he had no power to give them food or a
ticket, and that they should apply personally to the
two paid guardians, a Colonel Hograve and a Mr. Lecky,
who would hold a board meeting the next day in
Delphi Lodge, Bundorragha. The Lodge was situated in
the wildest, uninhabited region in Ireland, eighteen
miles distant from the proper boardroom at Westport,
and ten miles distant from Louisburgh. This was a
deliberate trap set up by the Government of that day
in order to decoy the starving Celts out to this wild
region in order to slaughter them.

These six hundred people had no homes to return to;
they were in rags, almost naked, and they had not tasted
any kind of food for days, so severe was the famine.
They sat down in front of the houses in Louisburgh
during that night, and many of them were found stark
dead where they lay next morning. On that day some
four hundred of them arose shivering in their rags, all
barefooted and still without food; they sighed and
looked up to heaven before setting out on a journey
from which none of them was to return.

When they reached Glankeen, they had to wade
through the river which was swollen by recent rains.
Their rags from the hips downward were saturated with
water on that cold, damp day. When they reached the
southern bank of this rapid mountain torrent, there was
nothing even resembling a road between that spot and
Doolough, so that they had to negotiate the dreadful
goat track along the brow of the precipice which overhangs the house of the late Captain Houstan. They
encountered another river far deeper than that of Glankeen, and since there were no bridges in those days
they had to battle their way through the stream, with
the result that they were wet to the waist.

When the wet and suffering peasantry reached Delphi Lodge, the vice-guardians were at lunch and could not be disturbed, so the people sat down in their damp, miserable rags among the pine trees, and there many of them expired. When the two gentlemen condescended to see the peasantry, they refused to grant them relief or tickets to the workhouse, so the fearful journey had been all in vain.

Night was now approaching and ten long, weary miles of a wild, uninhabited region lay between them and that land where once had stood their happy homes. Now they were homeless, and with despair in their hearts they set out once more for the place of their birth. When they reached the river where Houstan's house now stands, they once more had to wade through it, saturating their rags anew. The wind veered around to the north-west bringing a storm with showers of piercing hailstones. Their wet rags began to stiffen like cold sheet iron around their emaciated limbs, and soon they began to fall and die along the rough path, or to fall in their weakness into the lake below.

When they reached that terrible spot called the Stroppabue, on the very brow of the cliff, the tremendous squalls swept them by the score into the lake, and those who were trying to climb the steep-slanting pass or stroppa, lost their hold and fell as they climbed. The corpses which fell into the lake were never recovered The few who survived the struggle through the Stroppabue continued to fall and die until the last of them perished on the southern bank of the Glankeen river. On the next morning the trail from Glankeen to Houstan's house was covered with corpses as numerous as the sheaves of corn in an autumn field. There is nothing in Irish history to equal this horrible butchery, nor is there anything in the history of Europe to equal it in horror, save the tragic retreat of Napoleon's army from Moscow.

On the following day, the Relieving Officer took gangs of starving men with him from Louisburgh along the corpse-strewn trail, and they buried the slaughtered peasants without coffins just where they fell. When they reached Doolough there was no earth along the goat track deep enough for graves save in the little glen or ravine which ran down to the brow of the cliff, and which frowns above the dark lough just beside the terrible Stroppa-bue. So they had to gather all the corpses and carry them to the little glen where they buried them in pits just as on a battlefield, and there they lie sleeping where the sighing of the winds through the tall, wild ferns which wave above their nameless graves forever sings their requiem.

It was in this lonely glen in which so many of his former neighbours lay buried that Jimmy McDonough of the golden hair and the wonderful voice sat down to rest at midnight, unconscious of the savage, lonely scenery which surrounded him. His thoughts were turned to Connemara, that unknown region to the south, towards which he fled to escape the memories of his home and his shattered love.

The Rolling Stone of Lether Brickawn

As Jimmy McDonough sat at midnight in the lonely glen at Doolough where many of his former neighbours were buried, wondering what awaited him in his journey to Connemara, he was suddenly aroused from his lethargy by the shrill cry of a woman wafting its frightening way through the ravines of the ominous mountains. A cold thrill ran down his spine as he sprang up and fled along the rocky goat track, nor did he look behind him until he reached Bundorragha. The inhabitants of the well-sheltered, ancient hamlet were fast asleep as he went out on the quay and unmoored a boat. He took an oar in each hand and pulled vigorously across beautiful Killary Bay. When he reached the Galway side of the bay he securely moored the boat, fore and aft. He sprang out and climbed the rugged hill of Derry-na-Clough, and turning his face to the South, he sat down on a rock at the summit.

For the first time in his life he beheld the Irish Alps, the far-famed Banabola mountains, stretching away as straight as an arrow from the banks of the Corrib in the East to the shore of the wild western Atlantic, dividing the vast mountainous barony of Ballinahincha into two evenly divided halves. There they stood in their glory, all radiant and gorgeously decked out in their many-coloured summer holiday attire of purple-green and yellow, their white peaks shining with a silvery sheen as the early sun-rays glistened upon them. How to pass through or over these peaks was the problem which confronted Jimmy. But he was a resolute, lithe, vigorous young man who never was daunted by anything, so he determined to climb them, hoping that he would die in the effort, though not by his own hand, for he grieved deeply for his lost love.

Jimmy stood up and descended the southern slope of the rugged hill to traverse the green vale of Glencroff through whose centre there flows a charming river with low, verdant banks. As he crossed over this river he thought of Homer and the Scamander. When he finally emerged from the valley, some five miles of heath-covered moors lay between him and the Banabolas. As he advanced, he roused a covey of grouse and shot two of them which he took with him. He soon reached a deserted village called Letter-shan-balla which stood on the western slope of a heather-clad hill, a village whose inhabitants all perished of hunger some three years before.

When he reached the great monarch of the eastern range of the Banabolas, the stupendous Maamturk mountain which stands on the eastern shore of beautiful Loch Inagh, he met another deserted village nestling in a crevice beneath the northern base of the mountain; this place was called Lether Brickawn, and it was now abandoned, for all of its inhabitants had died of hunger. Here Jimmy lingered, for this ruined little hamlet had a history. When inhabited, it belonged to the parish of Ballinakill about the year 1825 or 1830.

The parish priest of Ballinakill and his two curates used to hold a confession station in the now deserted

village. One of the curates was a young man of great
strength and stature who was reputed to be the cleverest
young priest in the Archdiocese of Tuam for, through
his mother, he inherited natural talent, eloquence and
fluency both in Irish and English, for she belonged to
the O'Malleys of Curragaun, a village near the mouth of
the Killary. The O'Malleys were the wealthiest and most
eloquent stock who ever figured West of the Reek.

The young curate was Father James O'Malley of
Cahir, a village just beside the little town of Louisburgh.
When Archbishop McHale was translating Homer and
Moore, one of the priests anonymously attacked him
in the newspapers of that day, and the letters were as
galling to the Archbishop as the letters of Junius were
to those they were aimed at, but the Archbishop could
not learn the identity of his attacker. He called together
all the priests of the Archdiocese of Tuam, but again he
failed to find the identity of the culprit.

'Well, now,' said His Grace, 'the enquiry is over and
there are only two men among you fit to write such
able letters. No man ever wrote those letters but you,
James O'Malley, or you, Joe Burke.' Father Joe Burke
was then a young curate in Louisburgh. 'Well, Your
Grace,' said Father Joe, 'it is I who wrote the letters;
give me my exeat and I will leave your diocese.' So he
received it and went off to America. I have given this
anecdote in order to show how clever Father O'Malley
was and the opinion His Grace had of him. Big Father
James O'Malley of Cahir is, I daresay, quite forgotten
in his native parish, but not by me. He lies buried on
the bright, sunny slope above the holy well of Kilgeever,
with a Celtic Cross above him guarding the handful of
brown clay which was once a very distinguished, intel-
lectual priest.

When the confession station was ended in the little
village of Lether Brickawn on that day years ago, the
priests, as was usual in those days, remained for dinner.
Father James O'Malley determined to climb the tremendous Maamturk mountain which overhung the little
hamlet. Yet, it is easier to climb than Croagh Patrick,
although it is far steeper. This mountain was covered

with heath and wild mountain grass, and it was generally cloud-capped. When Father James reached the
summit, he saw an enormous granite rock on the very
brow of the mountain. At the least this rock was two or
three hundred tons weight, and it rested on a bank of
red clay. Since the earliest ages the sheep, goats and
other animals used to shelter beside it in winter time,
and in summer they used to seek its shade. They were
forever scraping and scratching themselves against the
bank on which the rock rested, so that as time went by
they wore away the clay, undermining two-thirds of
the base.

Father James saw that the rock was sure to fall with
the first rain or frost of the winter, and without a
thought of the little village which lay below the hill, he
determined to dislodge the stone for fun's sake. He lay
on his back, placed his feet against the rock, and with
might and main he gave a shove. Like some pre-historic,
monstrous animal aroused from its lair, the dreadful
rock sprang into life, and bounded down the side of the
mountain, driving a torrent of stones and pebbles before
it. As it sprang and collided against other rocks, the
echoes rang out with the shock of the impact.

The priest had forgotten the village, and as he searched the spot on which the rock had stood, he saw a bull's
horn embedded in the clay. It occurred to him that in
olden times the horn must have been shoved in through
a rat or weasel hole. When he picked up the horn to
examine it, he found within it twenty-five gold guineas.

Meanwhile, the villagers had been sitting below on a
hillock inhaling the sweet perfume which was wafted
towards them from the station house by the mild
zephyrs, for the air was redolent with the aroma of
roasting and boiling. All too soon they were aroused
from the pleasant occupation by the sound of a dreadful
crash high above them. Startled, they looked up and
saw death rushing down towards them. With might and
main they ran for dear life towards a foothill. On came
the rock, springing and bounding, gaining impetus as it
descended and soon, as if in a fury, it sprang into the
doomed little village of rude stone cabins, and it took

three of the houses with it into the deep, swampy glen
at the foot of the mountain.

When Father James descended the hill, singing one of
the old tunes, he found the village in ruins and the
natives lamenting. The wild, sad Irish wail of the homeless matrons rent the air, but the priest was not astonished at the ruin he had caused, for he sprang from a
race that never wondered at anything. 'Ah, my friends,'
he said, 'be of good cheer. It was God who put it in my
mind to cast down the stone, for it was sure to fall next
winter, perhaps when ye would be gathered at breakfast
or dinner, or when sleeping at night in your beds, when
ye would be sure to be killed. See what I found under
the rock,' and he showed them the horn and the gold.
'This will build new homes for you, far better than the
ones you have lost.' So he divided the contents of the
horn among them, and went off to dinner.

Then the villagers went to work with a will and soon
three new homes arose like phoenixes out of the ruins.
They were the envy of the other villagers, for such, alas!
is human nature; some of the inhabitants prayed fervently that Father James on his next visit would roll
down another rock and find another bull's horn full of
gold in order that they, too, might build more up-to-date
mansions.

The Bailiff and the Blacksmith

In the winter of the year 1825 all the peasantry who
dwelt along that portion of the southern shore of Clew
Bay which stretched westward from Old Head to
Emlagh, were gathering seaweed in a full storm which
was blowing from the north-west, accompanied by
terrible showers of hailstones. The sea was in a fury as
it lashed against the headlands, and the clouds seemed
to be surcharged with electricity as the heavens were
illuminated by great flashes of lightning. The thunder

crashed and shook the universe, rolling and tumbling as it died away in the distance.

About noonday as the toiling workers looked in the distance across the angry ocean they beheld a great ship coming in the sound which separates Clare Island from Achill, and they plainly saw that she was in distress. When she weathered the northern point of Clare Island at Carramore, the wind veered around some points towards the north, with the result that the ship was driven towards the west. It became evident to the watchers that she was heading for Polgloss, a little village which lies nestling at the foot of the western slope of the hill of Carramore.

All those who were working along the shore ran towards the little village. On she came, the noble ship, her white sails torn and streaming in the storm as she ran before the wind. Sometimes the watchers would lose sight of her as she sank buried in the trough of the sea between the breakers, but then she would appear once more, raised high on the white crest of a great roller, only to fall headlong with a crash almost on her beam ends, once more lost to view. On came the gallant ship, fighting and battling through the raging ocean towards the shore.

There were wild hurrahs from the crowd on land as the ship drew nearer and nearer. Suddenly, a strange thing happened, for the crew who were gathered in the bows of the vessel threw a cabin boy overboard into the raging breakers. Some brave men in the crowd of watchers caught each other's hands and waded out towards the little lad who was swimming weakly towards them, and they carried him safely to land. The great ship was lifted on high by the ground swell and driven headlong into the shingly beach or dourlin. The sailors were exhausted, but when they recovered they told their sad story.

Some two months before, while they were at sea, the captain lost his bearings and the ship had been wandering ever since. During those dreadful days they had not once glimpsed the sun or the stars. When windward of the Bills a wave struck the vessel and carried away the wheelhouse together with the captain who was steering the ship. When asked why they cast the cabin boy overboard, they said they thought they were approaching some part of the coast of Africa, and they feared the crowd on shore might be savages who would murder them. In order to test the crowd they threw the boy overboard, for if the people tried to save him they were sure to be Christians, but if they didn't try to save him they were sure to be savages. As the crew told their story the tide was receding, and in a short space of time the ship stood high and dry, nor was she much injured. She was laden with oranges packed in boxes. In the evening, each man of the crowd took home with him a box of oranges.

At that time the Brownes of Westport had a bailiff in Louisburgh, an Orangeman from the North who hated the Catholic peasantry and did them much harm, but he detested above all of them four men, one of whom was a blacksmith. The bailiff took charge of the ship until the arrival of the Coastguard, at which time he took some of the Coastguard with him to search for the boxes which the peasantry had taken away. This was a pretext to ruin his four enemies, for he began with them first of all. He tore down their gerlings of potatoes in their barns and let them loose over the threshed oats; he tore down their turf-stacks and their ricks of hay as well as all the stacks of corn and cocks of straw. In fact, he almost put them out of house and home, but then like a fool he attacked the blacksmith's property, and he even smashed his furniture.

The blacksmith when roused to fury was relentless and unforgiving, and he swore a terrible oath that he would see this business through to the bitter end. Everyone who knew the smith realized that it would be a fight to the finish. The smith fasted three days and three nights before he went out to his forge and took hold of his hereditary sledge, for he was a hereditary smith. He began to smith the cold, naked anvil, and the anvil began to roar until it rang out through the little town and the sound was heard in the adjacent villages. The peasantry knew from traditional instinct what was on, and the roar of the anvil as he smote it had something human in it, for it was like the roar of some gigantic mortal in the death agony. This diabolical thing was much dreaded by the Irish peasantry. From the earliest times they called it gratha an inune, that is, the thrashing of the anvil.

The people who heard the anvil roaring were much perturbed and retired early to bed that night. Next morning when they arose the news spread like luska sleiva that Jimmy Blain, the terrible bailiff, was a corpse. He was found sitting up in bed, his eyes wide open as if glaring at some fearful object, his teeth set rigidly, and his two hands grasping the bedclothes as if trying to strangle some demon. The news soon reached the three countrymen whose homes he had ruined. 'No,' said one of them, 'I will never believe it until I see the house fly walking on his dead face and going into his nostrils.' So they went to the wake where they saw the house flies on his face, and the incredulous one went home satisfied. I knew the smith, who died of a colic in 1848, but the other three men whom the bailiff ruined lived on until I was a young man, and I have heard them telling this story a hundred times. I never heard them describe the roaring of the anvil but I thought of Lia Fail or Stone of Destiny which roared beneath the monarchs of ancient Erin at their Coronation.

Hugh Gordon, the 'Jumper' of Feenone

Beneath the north-eastern slope of Mweelrea, a wild mountain in West Mayo, lies the sequestered village of Feenone which is far-famed for the fertility of its soil and the industry of its inhabitants who seemed to resemble the two races of mankind whom Gulliver met in his travels. But if they differed in physique they excelled as husbandmen, having at all times and seasons an abundance of the necessities of life. At eventide in

summer when the village maidens sat milking their
cows on the slope of the great hill which overhung the
hamlet, or along the verdant banks of the river which
placidly glides through it, their jocund songs filled the
vale with melody which denoted to the passing stranger
that they were a happy and contented peasantry. The
feathered songsters seemed to vie with the milkmaids,
for the melodious voice of the cuckoo resounded amid
the cliffs and ravines of the mountains; the thrushes
gushed forth their joyous songs in dark hazel bowers;
blackbirds were whistling in the evergreen holly; the
corncrakes were calling in the meadows and cornfields
which sloped down to the limpid stream, and the linnets
and other little warblers were twittering on the brambles. Such was the village of Feenone in the old times,
but alas, I fear the hand of time has now despoiled
and denuded it of much of its former embellishment, its
charming sylvan scenery.

The townland was laid out in rundale, a system
which is much criticized and condemned by modern
writers who pose as experts, and who would have the
people believe that it arose from or as a result of the
ignorance of our ancestors, but if we inquire into the
system we find that the opposite is the fact. Let us
suppose that twelve men rented a vacant townland in
order to build a village in which to live; we, of the
present day, might think they should divide the land
into twelve strips and then cast lots for them. But then
perhaps six of the men might have very good strips,
while the others might have very bad ones. Since this
would be against the rules of fair play, how did they
divide the townland? They divided it according to the
Brehon Laws laid down by Cormac McArt, making three
parts of the townland, that is, the very best land, the
middling land, and the worst land. Then they made
twelve parts of the best land and cast lots in order that
each would have a portion of the good land, and they
followed the same procedure for the middling land and
the poor land. The reader can see how fair, honest and
unselfish our ancestors were in dealing with each other.
Nor does this denote ignorance. There were no fences

except upright stones here and there to mark the mearings, and when the peasants harvested the last of their crops in November, the townland was common to all of the inhabitants until the following April.

The great hills which overhung the village and the vast moors which surround it were rent free and common to all the people the whole year round. This was the rundale system which came down to us from our pagan ancestors, and it exists on some estates where I now dwell down to this day. Strange to say, there was scarcely ever a dispute among the people over this system, but, of course, there is seldom a rule without an exception. I have gone into detail about this system in order that the reader may understand my story which, if rudely put together, is surely a sad one, a story which arose from a trivial cause and caused the ruin of a happy family, a story which need never have been told if the chief actor in it had obtained fair play and justice. Nor would I record this story now if any of the relatives of the leading character were now alive, but they are not, for the sept to which he belonged has been extinct in the male line for over half a century.

In that Arcadian village of Feenone there lived about the year 1830 a very respectable man named Hugh Gordon, a small farmer and a blacksmith. Since time immemorial, all his ancestors who dwelt in Carramore were hereditary smiths, and they were considered to be one of the most ancient tribes West of the Reek. The males of every generation seem to have been few in number, but the females became the ancestresses of one-third of the peasantry West of Old Head. Hugh Gordon was tall of stature, wonderfully broad-shouldered, and hideously pock-marked. Unfortunately for himself, he was a good scholar, considering the age in which he lived; in fact, he was a far better-informed man than any man of his class and status of the present age, but he lacked what he most needed in life, namely, patience and fortitude in bearing up against a wrong and an injustice.

About the year 1830, a dispute arose between Hugh and a neighbour as to the ownership of one of the little

patches of ground. I dare say that since there were no
fences the boundary marks may have become obliterated. Of course, there was much scolding and unpleasantness, and the two contestants went to law, but
when the county chairman failed to settle the case, he
sent it back to the Parish Priest to arbitrate it. The P.P.,
a Father Gibbons, was quite an old man, almost in his
second childhood, who thought very little of a small
bit of land in far-away Feenone, so without a thorough
investigation he decided against Gordon, although it is
quite certain that the land belonged in fact to Gordon.
Twenty years afterwards, when Gordon's name was on
every tongue, I heard all the old men of the region
declare that the land belonged to Gordon.

Hugh Gordon came of a race who never forgot or
forgave, a silent race. When Sunday came around, he
dressed himself in his best clothes and walked to Louisburgh where so many of his relations then lived. When
he reached the square, he turned to the left and walked
down to the Protestant Church and became 'a jumper'
in order to spite the priest, moryagh, and so his doom
was sealed. He had committed a crime and a sin against
nature, for he had done a thing which was unheard of
in that western region since the time when Saint Patrick
prayed and fasted on the summit of the blessed Reek; all
during that long period of fourteen hundred years a
western peasant was never known to desert the faith of
his fathers. For wasn't it the peasantry, the class to
which he belonged, who kept the Catholic faith alive in
Ireland from the days of Elizabeth down to the days of
O'Connell, and who supplied most of the priests who
guided the people on towards heaven? The grand, heroic
priests of penal times were sons of the same peasants
who were smuggled off to Spain to be educated and
ordained and then returned to Ireland, determined to
lay down their lives for the faith of their fathers. May
it be always remembered that if the keeping of the faith
lay with the Irish aristocracy and gentry, the Catholic
faith would have long since vanished, for the gentry of
Irish descent gave up the faith much sooner than those
of English descent, in order to retain their estates, or in

order to grab those of their neighbours. For instance, the O'Malleys of Belclare and of Murrisk 'jumped' and became Protestants sixty-two years before the Brownes of Westport became Protestants. The last of the pack-men of the West often told me that his uncle, Owen O'Malley of old Cahir-na-Mart, who reared him, frequently told him that he attended Mass in a large, barn-like structure which stood on the top of the hill of Carralurgan, and that it was one of the Brownes of Westport who used to serve Mass there, a young gentleman named Peter Browne Kelly, so we can see that the apostasy of the Brownes is of recent date.

When Hugh Gordon left the Protestant Church that Sunday morning, he found to his cost that he had severed all connection with his nearest and dearest friends and relations, as well as with the peasantry of the West. He had dug a chasm, a gulf, that could not be bridged over. He had done an unnatural deed, and now the people feared him as if he had suddenly become possessed by a devil; in fact, they suddenly became afraid of their lives of him as if he were some terrible man who had risen from the grave. As he walked down Bridge Street, Louisburgh, he saw all the doors closed against him; when he crossed the bridge and began to wend his way homewards, all those he overtook crossed themselves and fled through the fields or bogs, and those who were coming towards him did the same, for they were afraid of his pock-marked face.

When he reached his home in Feenone, he saw all the villagers blessing themselves and rushing towards their houses, and now he realized that he was a ruined man. Never, oh never, was he to hear their friendly voices welcoming him to their bright firesides. Never, oh never again would he feel the pressure of their friendly hands, for he had done a deed on that day which was unheard of in that region, and they were determined never more to associate with him. For a month he remained at Feenone as if in prison, and the loud, familiar clang of his anvil was hushed and stilled. Then he cast the doors of his once happy home open to the winds and fled to England. The outraged peasantry heaved a sigh of relief, for they imagined that they were rid of him for ever.

For twenty years Gordon remained in England until he was quite forgotten in his native parish. Then the great famine began. At that time there were fifteen hundred families in the Parish of Louisburgh, Kilgeever Parish, which was then thickly populated. It had a coastline which extended from Kilsallagh to the Killary, and from its mouth to Aasleagh at the head of the beautiful little bay, and every valley, glen and dell of that vast, mountainous region was thickly populated. One-third at least of the inhabitants were squatters, conacre men, who had no land or means whatever. When the potato, their staple food, failed, their doom was sealed. The first year of the famine they perished with hunger at the rate of at least two hundred persons each week. Then the mild, amiable parish priest lost heart, or at least his courage, for I dare say he thought the end of the world was at hand, so he asked for his exeat and fled away to far-off Buenos Aires in South America, leaving his perishing flock and poor old weeping Erin far behind him. When the famine cloud had rolled away, carrying with it two or three millions of the Irish peasantry, the old priest caught his courage with both hands and returned to the now denuded Isle of Destiny whose once emerald surface was now disfigured by the skeletons of ruined houses, and the nameless graves of his famished countrymen. It was assumed that he would never get a living from the great John McHale of Tuam, but it turned out otherwise, for shortly after his return he was quietly installed as P.P. of Clifden. When the old priest fled at the end of the first year of the famine, he was replaced by the much admired and respected Father Tom McCaffrey, a Westport man, who unfortunately was a chronic invalid suffering from consumption. Soon after his appointment, he lay down on his bed in Toureen, never to leave it again until he was carried to his grave in the old chapel of Louisburgh.

This critical time was the golden opportunity for the Irish Church Mission, the Protestant organization. They grasped their opportunity, and after a twenty years' absence they let loose Hugh Gordon among the starving peasantry of his native parish. He was accompanied by a strange parson and a large staff of scripture readers and ranting preachers, who came to preach the Word, as they called it. They looked around in order to choose a site on which to build the new Jerusalem, and they chose the village of Bunlehinch which lay along the northern margin of the charming vale of Cloonlara in the centre of the parish. The village was inhabited, but the then Marquis of Sligo was accommodating. To his eternal shame, he evicted the villagers and handed over Bunlehinch to the Irish Church Mission whose members began to build the colony, or new Jerusalem, at a great rate, and phoenix-like it soon rose out of the ashes of the ruined village.

A neat cottage was built for the manager, Gordon, the new Mahomed of the West, and soon there appeared a church with a schoolhouse, and a long street of cottages for the ' 'verts'. The cottages were soon filled, for hunger is a great leveller. When hunger comes in by the door, pride and shame fly out through the window. But even if some of the starving peasantry lost their pride and shame, they didn't lose the faith of their fathers. Gordon was cock of the walk, tricked out in the garb of a minister of the Gospel, and the air was filled with the ringing of bells and the singing of vespers.

Still, Gordon's lust for converts was unsatisfied. He determined to start an auxiliary colony, and of all the places in the parish he chose Bunowen, not that he expected converts there, but in order to annoy the parish priest who then lived in Bunowen. When Father McCaffrey died, he was succeeded by the venerable, saintly Father Myles Sheridan, another Westport man, who took up his abode in Bunowen. About the time when Father Sheridan was appointed, the famine was in its worst stage, literally mowing down the people. Their corpses were to be met everywhere, like dead thrushes after a great frost and snow, in the drains by the roadside, along the fences, in the fields, in fact, in the most unexpected places, for they went about in hun-

dreds seeking food, and as they went, they fell, never
to rise again, their faces as pale and thin as the face of
the moon when she first comes in. Young as I was then,
what I saw every day taking place all around me made
me as thoughtful as a full-grown person.

As young as I was, I came to the conclusion that
there were two distinct races of people in my native
parish at the time of the famine. One race I thought
was hardier than the other, and I cling to this opinion
still. The fair-haired, fair-skinned, freckled people were
a terrible sight to see. Their legs swelled, and the skin
broke around the calf of the leg and fell off their shins,
and from the fringes of skin there hung drops of yellow-
green water which trickled down their raw shins, a
dreadful sight to see. These fair-skinned people perished
about the fourth day of the fasting, but of course, long
before death they were worn to shadows, while I have
never seen the dark-haired, swarthy people in such a
state. The dark people fought a terrible battle for life.
They died about the sixth day of the fasting, and some
even lived for nine days, for I often listened to my
parents and others discussing this matter.

When Gordon determined to start a colony in Bunowen, it was then a village of thirty-three houses.
Twenty-three of these have been obliterated and have
vanished, and those who lived in them have been scattered by the four winds of heaven, but as I write I see
them clearly with the eyes of my mind. I see those
vanished houses and the ground on which they once
stood; I see the faces and forms of the people who
dwelt in them, and I hear the sonorous, loud-toned voice
of one of the men as clearly as when he sang the grand
old Irish love songs, a sad memory of the days that are
gone forever.

Beside the house in Bunowen where the priest then
lived, there is a bend towards the South in the road to
Louisburgh, and from that bend there ran a boreen
towards the East which met the road leading from
Long Street, Louisburgh, through the eastern portion of
Bunowen, and on through Balure Legan to Old Head.
On that end of the boreen, at the bend of the road

beside the priest's house, there stood for ages five houses inhabited by a little sept of the O'Gradys, who were nicknamed the Froukaghs, or Frenchmen, in consequence of their being fighters in the Galvanagh army. The old patriarch of the little sept, Tom Grady, was the grandest old peasant I have ever seen, and it was in his warm, bright kitchen, when I was a child, that I learned to love my native land, its glorious songs and legends, for Tom Grady every night in the year harboured some wandering, harmless beggarman or two, who were brimming over with songs and legendary lore, and we little chaps gloried in listening to these old men. His home, I dare say, was one of the oldest stone houses in the West, for any person who knew the manners and customs of the peasantry could read its age without asking a question. When an Irish peasant built his cot and went to reside in it, on the first St. Brigid's eve that came on, he made a small cross of timber or of straw and tacked it on the screw on the inside of the house, always on the right hand side as you entered the room, and on every St. Brigid's eve, from one generation to the next, a cross was tacked on the roof. All you needed to do to calculate the age of the house was to count the crosses tacked on the roof of Tom Grady's house.

These five houses of the O'Gradys were the vineyard of Naboth for which Gordon longed, in order to turn them into a 'jumper' colony close to the parish priest's cheek. Potter, the Louisburgh parson, and Gordon laid the matter before Lord Sligo who very kindly evicted the grand little sept and handed over their once happy homes to Gordon. The Gradys were banished forever from their ancestral homes and soon they became extinct, for they were scattered like chaff before the wind. These were the grand O'Gradys who at all times held open their friendly doors where weary travellers loved to call at this resting place of the wandering minstrel, this asylum of the forlorn mendicant; now there is not even a stone to mark the ground on which these homes once stood.

When the homes of the evicted O'Gradys were filled with converts, the parson and Gordon decided to give

them a beef dinner on the first Friday of their instal-
lation, an event at which all the elders of the church
were to preside, but when the savoury food was served,
not one of the converts would touch it, not even if they
were to be shot from a cannon's mouth. However, one
man who was nicknamed Tony Mirrish, a poor, starved
creature, longed for the meat, and I suppose that he
also wished to show the holy man that he was a true
convert. He ate the beef to repletion, but he paid the
penalty, for there was an eye that never sleeps looking
out from Heaven at the terrible example he was showing his almost famished, abstemious comrades.

Before an hour passed, Mirrish swelled to the bursting
point, and what do you suppose he did? He began calling
loudly in his native language for the priest, and the
parson, Gordon, and the rest of them were astounded.
'Ah, ma curp agus monam urth !' he shouted to his
pale, careworn wife, 'run for the priest, run, a clyra, if
ever you ran and bring me the priest !' She sprang up,
casting her conversion to the winds, and ran to Father
Myles who lived just beside them, and casting herself
at his saintly feet, she told him all with tears streaming
down her cheeks.

Father Myles was too prudent to be caught in a trap,
for he knew that if he went by himself the parson, Gordon and the strange preacher might murder him. He sent
for two of his neighbours, men who during the famine
acted the part of Tobias, the elder, in burying the dead.
They gathered the men of the village who accompanied
the priest to the sick man's house where they thrashed
the parson, Gordon and Company, and trampled them
in the gutter. The priest anointed the unfortunate man
who lingered in great agony for about a week, for in
going and returning from a hedge school which was held
in the town we little chaps used to stand at the bend
of the road, listening to his dreadful shouts.

When Tony Mirrish died, there was another pitched
battle for his corpse, for all the forces of the new
Jerusalem of Bunlehinch were gathered in order to have
the grave of a convert to show to visiting officials.
When they reached the bend in the road where the

boreen met it and where there was always a large flash
of water, Father Myles and the villagers met them.
There the battle began, and soon the parson, Gordon
and the preacher lay wounded and wallowing in the
ensanguined little, shallow lake. It was like a struggle
of the angels of light and the angels of darkness over
which would possess an immortal soul, but, as usual,
the angels of light triumphed and the villagers bore the
coffin to Carramore Strand and buried it in the now
obliterated sandbanks. Why there was no prosecution
I often wondered, but I dare say that no petty sessions
were held in Louisburgh in those days, or if they were,
I never heard of it, although there was another kind of
court held there once a month.

This court, presided over by a paid official called a
Seneschal, was called a Brehon Court, and it came down
to us from pagan times. The Seneschal was something
like an R.M. of our times, but I think his salary came
out of the county rates. His power was limited, for in
all cases, no matter how trivial, he had to have a jury of
twelve men to assist him. The Brehon Court was held in
a room on the ground floor of Grandy O'Donnell's house
and existed until about the year 1850. I believe this
was the last of its kind held in Connacht. The Seneschal,
whose name was John Burke, was a fine man in the
prime of life. He was also coroner of the district and
lived in the parish of Bekan. When we got an hour to
play, we went into the court in order to see the
Brehons in full session, and there we often stood looking at them with astonishment like Brennus and his
Gauls gazing at the senators of ancient Rome, and in our
juvenile opinion these men seemed to conduct their
deliberations with much dignity and decorum, for never
was there a sentence of death pronounced in that
ancient, merciful court.

About the year 1853 all the bogus converts fled from
the colonies like rats from a ship on fire, and every one
of them returned to the faith of their fathers, ungrateful
converts after all the stirabout or bruchawn they had
consumed for seven or eight years on the saintly Irish
Church Mission ! Then it was revealed that the Mission

had exhausted its funds, nor was this to be wondered at, for its adherents had squandered millions in feeding hypocrites and in building colonies, towns, in fact, in every parish along the shores of the wild Atlantic from Achill to Dingle, and in hundreds of other places too, and now they had nothing to show for this enormous outlay save hundreds of ruined, empty buildings whose smokeless chimneys became the breeding grounds of flocks of jackdaws.

In the days of his old age, Gordon got his mittimus, for the work was a failure, and he was given to understand that his services were no longer needed. Then the sensation of that age set in, for the news spread that Gordon would be at Mass next Sunday and would read his recantation, and all the people were overjoyed. When Sunday came around, and Father Michael Curley, who had succeeded the late Father Sheridan, had finished Mass, Gordon came out of the sacristy, stood on the altar, and read his recantation, following which he delivered a very penitential address.

There stood Hugh Gordon in his old age, erect, tall and gray, a man of grand physique. As I, a small chap, gazed at him, my heart bled to see his humiliating, forlorn condition, and I thought that those who by their greed and folly had caused his fall would have much to answer for. He was the grandest old man I ever beheld. The priest announced that there would be a collection held in that church and in the church of Gowlawn that day week, and the people took it up with much enthusiasm so that when the next Sunday came, both collections amounted to forty-six pounds, which was handed over to Gordon.

When this sum was spent, he was too proud to beg, so he walked over to Westport and entered the Workhouse where he died in a short time. His sad story shows us two things clearly; first, how cautious and careful men ought to be who are chosen to arbitrate in a dispute between neighbours, before they give a final decision, for if the trivial dispute I have recorded had been wisely handled, Gordon might have lived and died what he was in the beginning, a most respectable and very much respected man. His story also shows what dreadful results may follow from the act of a man who by foul means grasps the little field or vineyard of his neighbour, Naboth.

The Adventures of Foranan O'Fergus, the Physician

About the beginning of the seventeenth century there dwelt near the village of Borus a man named Foranan O'Fergus, and the little green toonagh or hillock where he lived, located between Borus and Forigil at the foot of the brown hill of Cuck-a-Kishawn, is called even to this day Auththie Foranan, which means the place of Foranan's house; surely O'Fergus must have left his footprints deeply imprinted on the sands of time when the name of the glen in which he lived is handed down to posterity.

This old man was a medical doctor, for the O'Ferguses were for at least five hundred years the acknowledged hereditary physicians of the Western Owls of the O'Malleys. They were all skilled leeches, for they had to undergo a rigid course of training from their fathers who kept a careful record of all the cures each effected during his lifetime, together with notes of how he treated the various cases of different maladies which came to his notice and which he cured, as well as the peculiar cases in which he was not able to effect a cure. These valuable records were written by hand, generally in Irish, and sometimes in Latin, for the art of printing was not in vogue in those days in the far West. The reader can see from the foregoing that the O'Ferguses weren't quacks, but were learned physicians. They were a small tribe or clan and don't seem to have been a prolific race, but they were far-famed, the males for their fine, masculine physique and florid complexions, the females for their beauty and feminine grace and winsome ways.

In the days I write about, the great valley which
environs the little town of Louisburgh in West Mayo
was all covered by a primeval forest so dense that if a
man mounted a tree branch at Fairy Hill on the seashore at Bunowen, he could travel from branch to
branch without touching the ground until he reached
Glan Bawn, a distance of at least six miles. The grandparents of the present writer saw it in the state I have
described when they were children. How it was denuded
of its timber in such a short period is astonishing to me,
but it can be accounted for by the fact that the invaders,
the Brownes, the Binghams and the Palmers, cut down
the woods in which the rightful owners, whom they
called Rapparees, were concealed, for well they knew
their lives were in danger until the woods were cut
down.

On a certain day in summer, Foranan O'Fergus received two urgent calls, one from the bleak, storm-
swept village of Cloonthie, some distance West of the
charming vale of Cloonlara, where a man lay danger-
ously sick, and the other to visit three young men who
lived in a little ravine called Dereen-an-Albanagh, on
the banks of Killary Bay, about a mile or two distant
from its mouth, and who had been grievously wounded
in a very peculiar manner. When Foranan had breakfast,
he began to prepare to set out. He took down his
Bireath or Baret cap, a Celtic headgear which resembled
a Turkish turban; as usual he blessed himself by making
the sign of the cross before he placed the cap on his
head.

Next he took down his skean dhu which hung on its
scabbard on the wall of his bedchamber and he hung it
on his right hip, for in those days no man dared go
abroad without it for the woods were infested with wild
hogs, wolves, and enormous wildcats. He put on his
kothamore or Celtic cloak, the most becoming garment
I have ever seen on the back of a tall, well-shaped man.
I dare say this garment is now extinct, for I haven't
seen one in over sixty years. O'Fergus next caught hold
of his Kleagh alpeen or alpinstock, a pole about six feet
long, sharpened on one end, which our ancestors used

for hill climbing. He called to his side Flann, his great wolfhound, blue-coloured, coarse-haired and brown-eyed. He was thoroughly equipped for the journey as he crossed his threshold and disappeared through the wild woods. His wife, who had De Danann blood in her veins and who retained some of their superstitions, caught a live coal with the tongs and cast it on the floor in a peculiar manner. If the tongs when cast opened wide it boded good, but if the tongs did not open to the full extent, this boded evil. She cast the coal skilfully, but the tongs didn't open, and her heart sank within her, for well she knew by the unlucky omen that the partner of her joys and sorrows would encounter many dangers before she clasped him again to her white, throbbing bosom.

Foranan held on his way towards the West and soon issued from the woods at Tully. He crossed the river with his faithful Flann by his side, climbed Run-na-hallya and traversed the great moor called Ru-na-goppal; soon he reached Furmoyle, once the happy hunting ground of the far-famed Fena of Erin. He continued on through Carra-an-Iska and the charming vale of Cloon-lara, and soon reached Cloonthie where he entered the humble home of Roger O'Toole who lay on his death bed. When he entered the dark, rude cabin, many of the old men of the village followed him, for they wished to salute their hereditary physician.

The doctor examined the wounded man, and then turned towards the villagers to ask, 'This man must have got a fall from some tremendous height or cliff, so pray tell me, Toby Stanton, how did it happen, for his spine is broken, and he has but three days to live.' 'Musha, doctor,' said Stanton, 'he did get a great fall, and it was all his own fault for he would not be advised by us, for although a small man he was always headstrong and contrary, and now this is the end of it and I often told him so, for he would fight with his nails, and yet he was a good neighbour, the cunning creature. 'About two months ago,' he continued, 'O'Toole sent his fine mare grazing on the wild mountains of Mweel-rea, and his son went out to see her each Sunday, and she was coming on fine. Last Sunday when the boy went to see her, she was dead in Lugatharee on the shore of Doolough, at the foot of the great cliff, cast down by the eagles. There she lay on the broad of her back and with her neck broken, so the son returned weeping and told his father. The father got into a rage and swore he would have it out with the eagles. The next morning he took down his skean dhu and hung it on his hip; next he took a brown flannel quilt which he rolled up and placed under his arm, and he set out for Doolough, some five miles distant from his home. We followed him, for we knew something terrible was going to take place.

'When we reached the Glan Cullin on the western shore of the lake, we saw the dead mare in the deep, dark glen of Lugatharee, at the foot of the great cliff. We lay in ambush under the wide, spreading holly trees while O'Toole went on towards the dead animal. He drew his skean and ripped her open as she lay on her back. He removed the entrails and hid them, and then he wrapped the old quilt around him and lay down in the cavity of the carcass. Suddenly a strange thing happened, and the climax came sooner than we had expected, for two great eagles floated down from the cliff and alighted on the carrion. O'Toole stretched forth his right hand and took hold of the leg of one of the eagles above the talons, while with his left hand he caught the other eagle in a similar manner. The sacred monsters arose with a scream and took wing, carrying O'Toole with them, for the brave little Celt held on to them like grim death.

'There was a strong wind blowing which helped them to soar aloft towards their home in the terrible precipice. O'Toole must have realized his terrible position as he hung in the air between heaven and earth, for well he knew they would tear him to pieces or cast him headlong into the dark chasm. When they had raised him a hundred feet in the air, he loosened his grip and fell with a great crash on his back on the soft morass. We rushed towards him, but we found him stark dead, so we cut down some roan saplings which grew among

the holly in the glen, and of these we made a rude litter
on which we carried him home with much grief. When
we reached home, we found to our astonishment that he
had life in him and could take a sup, and it was then,
doctor, that we sent for you,' concluded Stanton. 'Well
now,' said Foranan, 'send for your parish priest, Father
David Lyons, to anoint him and prepare him for eternity, for he has only three days to live.' 'We will send
for him, but it's hard to locate him,' said Stanton, 'for
you know he has no house or home of his own, and
never had.' 'I know that,' said Foranan.

Father David Lyons was born in the village of Kella-
doon, midway between Killary Bay and the present
town of Louisburgh. When he was twenty years old,
he went to Spain and entered the College of Salamanca
where he remained until he was ordained a priest, and
then he returned to Ireland to be appointed by the
Archbishop of Tuam as parish priest of Kilgeever, his
native parish. He never had a curate, for although he
was a small man, he possessed more than one man's
share of strength and vigour. While he was in Spain he
never met a man fit to wrestle him, nor did he ever
meet one in Connacht fit to wrestle him either. Until
the day of his death he never had a house or home, but
went about from village to village, sleeping in the
houses of the country people, on some straw in a
corner of the kitchen, for he didn't know at what
moment he might have to spring up and rush to the
mountains for safety, for the priest hunters were
abroad in the land in those days. He never accepted
dues, save what should go to the bishop; he never had
a farthing in his pocket, or in a box or a trunk, for he
never had a box or trunk.

He always wore a body coat, vest, and breeches of
black frieze, a strong pair of brogues over which he
wore a pair of knitted spatters, all of which he got
from the people, but although he was dressed in this
humble garb, when he took out his stole, and kissed it,
and placed it around his neck, he could dry up the Red
Sea or bring down Manna from heaven. He lived to be
a great age, and he was vigorous to the last. He died in

his native village, and he lies slumbering in a nameless
grave in Killeen in the charming vale of Cloonlara,
where perhaps his slumbers are as serene and tranquil
as those of any canon or other dignitary of the Church
who might leave eight or ten thousand pounds behind
him to some worthless relatives who may never offer
up a prayer for the repose of the soul of the benefactor
who left them the windfall.

Leaving Roger O'Toole to the ministrations of Father
David Lyons, Foranan departed and set out for the banks
of the Killary, and as the shades of evening were
beginning to descend he reached his destination and
entered the dark, rude cabin of Ulick Burke, whose
three stalwart sons were grievously wounded and disfigured, for each of them had lost half a nose. Foranan
stood in the cabin, spellbound and appalled. 'How in the
world did this happen, pray tell me at once,' he said.
'Oh no, not until you have partaken of some refreshments,' answered the old man, 'for it is a long and sad
story.' The old woman got up and handed him a noggin
of boiled new milk sweetened with honey, into which
was poured two glasses of poteen or iska baha, and
when he had taken this strengthening beverage, he sat
down to dinner.

At the conclusion of the meal, the oldest son began
to relate his sad story. 'About a week ago,' he said,
'I went to bed just after saying the Rosary, and I fell
into a tranquil sleep, but about the dead hour of the
night a Naugh stood at my bedside.' [To enlighten the
present-day reader who may not know what a Naugh
is, let it be said that it is a friendly kind of ghost of
whom the peasantry were not afraid, for the Naugh
came to tell the sleeper where he would find a hidden
treasure.] 'The Naugh stood at my bedside and said to
me, "Go to the lake of Althor which lies beneath the
northern bank of the rugged hill of Derrygoriv. There
you will see a firm turfbank, and when you reach the
centre of this bank, stretch on your stomach and look
beneath you into the lake. There you will see about two
feet of the bogdale tree which is embedded in the bog
protruding into the water; look closely at it, and then

you will see a pot hung by a pothook on it, just as if it hung over a fire. The pot is filled to the cosheen with gold, but around the cosheen you will see coiled an enormous serpent which is nothing more or less than the spirit of the dead miser who hoarded up this gold. Then insert your gaff under the pothooks, lift up the pot and with all speed run towards the stream which divides two townlands; jump across it with the pot, the spell will be broken, and the gold is yours.'

'The Naugh came to my bedside the second and third nights, repeating the same advice, so on the next morning I took a strong gaff with me and set out for the lake. When I reached it, I made for the northern bank and began to investigate in order to locate the pot. Sure enough, I saw it hanging on the beam some six feet below the surface. Then I stretched on my stomach in order to catch hold of the pothooks with the gaff and lift up the pot, and then the serpent looked up at me with her terrible green eyes, and at once I became fascinated and helpless as an infant. Nor could I move hand or foot, but kept looking at it spellbound until it stiffened itself, reached up and deliberately bit off half my nose and disfigured me for life. Then my two other brothers attempted to lift the pot, but each was fascinated and spellbound, so each of them also lost half a nose.' 'Well,' said the doctor, 'I am unable to furnish you with new ones; all I can do is to give you some ointment which will soon heal the wounds. Just rub it on like vaseline or Zam Buck, and in a few days you will be all right.'

The next morning, Foranan arose early and determined to climb the western brow of the great mountain in order to take a short cut to his home in the East. He didn't need to climb to its apex, but only to the table land beneath the great cone. Even this climb was a task which would have deterred Hannibal in his best days, but the doctor was bound that he would surmount all obstacles and achieve his goal. He caught hold of his kleagh alpeen or climbing pole and began to climb the southern side of the great mountain of Mweelrea which bulges out and overhangs the waters of deep Killary

Bay, for he had learned climbing since his earliest youth, and he had a nerve as strong and a step as firm and sure as that of an Alpine Ibex, and as he climbed his ever-faithful Flann kept close beside him. When he had climbed some fifteen hundred feet, he reached the plateau or table land which stretched away from South to North, the whole breadth of the hill, as vast and undulating as an American prairie. He held on his way towards the North.

When he had traversed about two-thirds of the table land, he came to a lake which tradition states is inhabited by a fiend, or by many fiends. This lake is called Lough Cum, or the lake of the hound, and it is supposed to have the most beautiful gravelly shores of any lake in Ireland. Tradition says that if a man stood on the shore and challenged the lake to send up a champion to fight him, the lake would produce a champion. Or if a man called upon the lake to send up a dog to fight his dog, the lake would send up a black hound who would rend his dog.

Foranan did a deed of folly which he had cause to regret until the day of his death, for in order to test the legend, he called on the lake to send up a hound to fight Flann. No sooner had he uttered the words than the great black hound arose out of the lake and the fight began. It lasted from noonday until the sun was fast waning towards the West, and Flann was torn and wounded in many places, and his life was fast ebbing away. Then the lake hound caught him by the throat and sprang into the lake with the wolfhound's thrashing form, never to rise again. Foranan smote his breast, realising that with his inquisitiveness and folly he had lost his ever-faithful friend, a friend who so often hazarded his life in order to save his master, and now he was gone forever, the true and brave Flann.

With despair in his heart, Foranan fled down the deep declivity of the mountain, leaving that lake of demons far above him. He reached the lowlands between Doogan Hill and the little hamlet of Shraugh Rusky, six miles across the level moors from his home. He began to traverse the vast moor which stretches north-

ward from Glankeen and Derryfeach and trends downward towards the villages of Lachta, Shraugh-na-lusid,
and Shraugh-na-cliha. When he reached the centre of
the moor he encountered a lake, a portion of which
was overgrown with tall bulrushes, while the other
portion was covered with beautiful white water lilies
which glinted and sparkled in the summer evening sunshine. When he drew near the eastern shore of the lake,
above which grew a shrubbery of sally, hazel and yew
trees, he saw a sight which appalled him, a wild hog
running towards him. It was a sow who had just
farrowed a litter of young ones, and who had heard his
footsteps long before he had seen her, and now he knew
his end had come. Oh, if he had Flann, the brave and
fearless Flann would rend and tear her to pieces, but
Flann was lost through his own fault.

He stood there unarmed and defenseless. It is true he
had his knife, but well he knew he was no match for the
sow at close quarters, for she would rend him with her
horrible tusks. He signed himself with the cross and
bade farewell to hope, although he was no craven, but
an intrepid, dauntless man. He determined to fight to
the death with the weapon he carried. He took hold of
his climbing pole with both hands, as you would a
spear or lance. It was of wild mountain holly, as firm
and hard as iron, and sharp-pointed on one end. When
the rabid monster drew near him, open-mouthed, he
drove his alpinstock with all his strength and vigour
into her mouth and it went through her neck behind
the ear. He drew out the weapon suddenly, and the
sow's lifeblood gushed forth in torrents from the
wounds. She fell with a great splash into the lake below
and sank forever, and from that day to ours the lake is
called Lough-na-Muicka, or the lake of the pig.

Foranan looked up with gratitude to heaven for his
escape from a cruel death by the skin of his teeth, and
then resumed his journey. He soon reached Shraugh-
na-lusid and crossed the great river which could well be
named the little Nile, for from its source beneath the
great mountain of Curwock at Sachta it winds its way
through fertile plains until it discharges its waters into

Clew Bay at Bunowen. When he crossed the river, night
had set in, that is, if a midsummer's night should be
called night —

> 'For the sun loves to pause, with so fond a delay,
> That the night only draws a thin veil o'er the day.'

However, the witching hour of the night had come,
and the evil one was abroad seeking whom he might
devour. When Foranan drew near his home, he met a
sluggish mountain stream in which there was no ford.
All pedestrians passing that way had to leap across the
river. Just as the doctor reached the proper spot for
jumping, some huge, dark object stood on the opposite
bank, barring his progress. Foranan went along the
stream until he found another spot where he could
jump, but again the great beast confronted him. Again
he retreated to the proper place for jumping, but the
great beast lurked on the other side. He tried several
spots, but always with the same result. Then Foranan
knew that this was a fiend who sought to exhaust him
in order that he would perish on the bleak moor.

Determined to fight once more for his life, Foranan
took off his baret cap and blessed himself. He drew his
skean dhu out of its sheath, made the sign of the cross
on the blade, and then with the bound of an enraged
panther, he sprang across the stream and buried his
skean dhu to the hilt in the vitals of the demon. A voice
croaked forth from the huge, hairy body, imploring,
'Good man, draw out your knife and give another stab.'
'Oh no,' answered Foranan, 'one stab is sufficient, for
tradition says that if a man draws his knife out of a
demon, the fiend will then slay him.' He left his skean
dhu in the vitals of the demon and turned away. When
he knocked at his door and his wife cast it open, she
saw that his eyes were closed, and she realised that he
had encountered a fiend, so she led him by the hand to
a straw armchair beside the fire. From the saltbox which
hung on the wall above his head she administered to
him three pinches of salt in the name of the Trinity.
Her husband opened his eyes, the danger of fainting
now being removed.

Foranan remained in bed for two days and nights in order to recuperate, but on the morning of the third day he arose with the dawn in order to take his usual walk in the forest. When he reached an open glade he saw an enormous wolf approaching, limping on three legs. The doctor continued to advance towards the lame animal and when they met in the centre of the glade, the wolf looked up at him and began to whine as if beseeching him to look at the paw which he held out. Stooping down, Foranan examined it and found the central ball or heel greatly inflamed and charged with corruption. He took out his lancet and lanced it so that a vast quantity of matter was discharged. 'Now,' he said, 'my noble animal, come with me to the little rivulet and I will wash your wounded foot.'

The wolf followed him, and as the doctor was washing the wound he saw a great thorn embedded in the heel, so he drew this out with his forceps and bound up the wound. 'Meet me here each morning for fifteen mornings,' he said to the wolf, 'and I will wash your wound.' For fifteen mornings they met, and on the fifteenth morning Foranan said, 'Now, my noble wolf, you are quite healed, and you need not come anymore.' They parted, and the doctor did not see the wolf for many months. But when Foranan opened his door early one morning, there sat the wolf on the street, and he presented the doctor with three meel cows, and each cow with a calf. The wolf departed and was never seen again. The cows thrived well and increased and multiplied; they became such favourites among the peasantry that a proverb was originated which said : 'Never buy a meel cow, never sell a meel cow, but never be a day of your life without a meel cow.'

Deaf Hugh O'Fergus and his Descendants

When Foranan O'Fergus died and was carried up to Paradise, his mantle fell on the shoulders of his only son, Doctor Owen Bawn O'Fergus, who migrated from the foot of the brown mountain of Knock-a-Kilshawn and built his home in the great oak primeval wood of Collacoon, which was then the only wood left standing in the West. The remains of this dark wood exist to this day, and portions of the granite walls of Owen Bawn's house were to be seen almost on the mearing between Collacoon and the little village of Gurthalisheen, adjacent to the present town of Louisburgh; this old ruin was always called 'Balla Owen Bawn O'Faries', which means Owen Bawn O'Fergus's wall. This man must have lived a quiet, retiring life, for there is very little about him in the traditions or folklore of the region. All that is recorded is that he had four sons and one daughter, named Una or Winifred O'Fergus, of whom I shall speak further on.

When Owen Bawn's family grew up, three of his sons went on board a smuggling lugger at Old Head and were carried away to France where they entered a monastery, and after an absence of seven years they returned to Ireland on board another lugger and landed at Murrisk. They were then three Augustinian Friars, Father Ned, Father Owen Bawn and Father Owlan O'Fergus. They entered the old Abbey of Murrisk and lived and died there. I could not find the English translation of 'Owlan' for my Shanachie was an Irish-speaking man, although he was considered the best Shanachie of his day or since in the Province of Connacht. Under his tutelage I spent nine years, nor do I regret it.

The fourth son was named Hugh, and in the traditions and folklore of the country he is always called 'Aoidh Bour', which means deaf Hugh, but whether he was deaf I could not find out. He was the last and greatest doctor of his race. When he had learned all that his father could teach him of medicine, he set out for Scotland and entered the University of Edinburgh where he took his degrees. Then he was appointed a professor in the College where he remained for twelve years, at the end of which time he decided to return to his native land.

Just then his native parish of Kilgeever, which I now call Louisburgh, was about to undergo a drastic change, for the last of the Lords Mayo died, leaving no male issue of his son to succeed him. The title fell into abeyance, and was not revived for a generation or two. The widow of the last Lord Mayo of Tibod-na-Mung's breed, the Burkes, married Edmund Jordan of Old Head. She had a daughter by Lord Mayo who had married a Dublin carpenter named Lambert. Since it was a love match, they were poor. Mrs. Lambert gathered all the records she could put her hands on of the family and estate and sold them and her own claim to the estate, if she had a claim. She sold them for a few pounds to the first Lord Altamount, of Westport, who at once took forcible possession of Lord Mayo's vast property West of Croagh Patrick.

Since the days of Tibod-na-Mung until the death of the last Lord of his race, the Lords Mayo held a country seat at Askalaun, some two miles west of the town of Louisburgh, where they spent much time each summer. The mansion stood on the very spot on which now stands the home of Mr. Pat Durkan, and some of the flowers of Lord Mayo's garden bloomed annually in Mr. Durkan's garden when I was a lad. In this lodge during the life of the last Lord, there lived a younger scion of the Mayo family who was the rightful heir, and who became a claimant to the title and estate. This Burke was poor and friendless; Browne of Westport, his opponent, was rich and influential, but still it was the evidence of the hereditary bailiff of the property which was to decide the law suit. I dare say that the point at issue was Burke's pedigree. Tradition says that when the trial took place, the bailiff thought it wise to stick to the rich man, so he perjured himself in favour of Browne, and Burke was defeated.

A generation later, the son of the first claimant put forward his claim to the title and estate, and again it was the bailiff's evidence which was to decide the law

suit, but this was the son of the bailiff who had given
false evidence in the first case. The bailiff had a full-
grown daughter who was a charming peasant girl, and
the young claimant offered to marry this girl if her
father would give straight, honest evidence at the trial,
but the bailiff refused. He gave evidence in court in
favour of Browne, and when he was asked why he did
this, he replied, 'Did you want me to make a liar and a
perjurer of my father in his grave?' Young Burke lost
the property, and the bailiff's daughter lost the chance
of becoming Lady Mayo. I had the pleasure of being
acquainted with this young lady when I was a young
man. She was a grand old Irish matron who was always
called Aunt Kitty by her neighbours. She was alive when
I left West Mayo.

When Browne took possession of the property, one
of the first things he did was to send his bailiffs who
seized Owen Bawn's cattle for rent which Owen did not
owe him. Whether he owed it to Lord Mayo I do not
know. The bailiffs drove the cattle to Cahir-na-Mart,
and old Owen followed his stock, lamenting and ex-
claiming, 'Oh, I wish Aoidh Bour could hear about this
in Scotland!' He continued repeating it as he went
along, and it became a household word ever afterwards
in the West, for if two neighbours were scolding, the
people would say that Deaf Hugh could hear them in
Scotland.

As the bailiffs were descending the northern slope to
the hill towards Cahir-na-Mart, they were confronted
by a strange gentleman on horseback who said, 'You
have driven the cattle too hard, you have them almost
killed, for they are panting and frothing. To whom do
they belong?' 'They belong to Owen Bawn O'Fergus of
Collacoon,' they replied. Then the stranger dismounted
and looked around him until he saw a spring trickling
from the foot of a green hillock. 'Get me a loy and
shovel,' he said to some of the men who had gathered
around him, and they did. At his direction, they dug a
well, cleaned it up, and it immediately filled and the
stranger gave water to the cattle.

That much-neglected well is the most historic well in

the West of Ireland and should be as sacred as a shrine
to the people of Westport, for it is the last souvenir of
old Cahir-na-Mart now in existence. The strange gentleman who dug the well was Deaf Hugh O'Fergus, who
had returned to his native land, and the well bears his
name, being to this day called 'Tubber Aoidh Bour',
which means Deaf Hugh's Well, a name which is
familiar to the ears of the inhabitants of Westport, for
they have heard it uttered every day since their childhood. Now, as I have given them its history, I hope
they will pay more attention to this historic, much
neglected, ancient spring, the last landmark of old times,
and I'm sure they will look after it, for there is not to
be found in Ireland a man who loves his native town
and its surroundings more dearly than a Westport man.

When Deaf Hugh gave his father's cattle a drink, he
paid what Browne demanded. Then he placed his weeping old father, Owen Bawn, on horseback, and they
drove the cattle home to Collacoon where Hugh began
to practice his profession. On a certain day he was
called to attend a sick person in Askalaun, and after he
had attended the man and was on his way home, he
turned in to see a friend who lived just beside the lodge
in which lived Mr. Burke, the claimant of the Mayo
title and estate.

Hugh's friend, Mrs. Durkan, boiled him a posset, the
usual midday treat in those days, for there was no such
thing as porter or whiskey knocking about in peasants'
houses in those days when our ancestors were far more
temperate and abstemious than we are. Mr. Burke of the
lodge next door had three grown daughters, very beautiful young ladies. On that glorious summer's evening, one
of the young ladies was taking in some linen which was
spread on the blackthorn shrubbery, and she was singing
in Irish one of those grand old Connacht love songs.
'Musha, Dr. Fergus,' said Mrs. Durkan, 'isn't she the
finest singer you ever heard?' The doctor replied, 'She
is a charming young lady, surely, and she has a charming soprano voice, but wouldn't you be astonished if
you heard tomorrow morning that she was dead?' 'Oh,
the Lord save us, Doctor, what's that you're saying? The

cross of Christ between us and all harm !' exclaimed the
woman. The doctor returned home, and the first news
Mrs. Durkan heard in the morning was that Miss Burke
was found dead in her bed. Deaf Hugh wasn't a quack,
but a doctor, and he was the last doctor of his race.

I mentioned that Owen Bawn O'Fergus had a daughter
named Una or Winifred Fergus, who married the famous
smuggler, Shemus Fodda O'Malley, of Carramore. These
brave smugglers of the West deserve a word, in passing,
for they did more for Ireland during the terrible penal
times than any other race or class of Irishmen I know.
It was those brave smugglers who kept Ireland supplied
with priests for a period of two hundred years, for without the smugglers the country would surely have had
no priests. When the Tudors, and those who succeeded
them, smashed up the trade which was carried on between the great seaport towns of Ireland and Continental nations, the peasantry along the seashore from Kerry
to Donegal took up the business. Every man worth his
salt along that coast built ships of about seventy tons,
called luggers on account of their rig, and they did a
vast trade with France, Spain, Holland, and the Channel
Islands.

At that time, no man could enter a school or college
in Ireland in order to become a priest, so all the young
men of the Midlands who wished to become priests
made for the western seashore from which they were
quietly carried by the brave smugglers to France and
Spain, where they were freely educated and ordained
priests. They returned to their native land secretly on
board some smuggling craft. These men could never
have become priests were it not for the loyal smugglers.
When they returned to Ireland, these wonderful priests
of the penal times put on the garb of the peasants. They
needed to disguise themselves, for there were priest-
hunters who got five pounds from the infernal Sir John
Bingham of Castlebar for every priest's head they
brought him. There he sat, watching and waiting to
receive a priest's head like Herod waiting to receive the
head of St. John the Baptist from his dancing daughter.

When the young Spanish priests, as the peasantry

called them, for generally they were educated at Salamanca, the favourite Alma Mater of the youth of the
West, put on their peasant garb, each one took his life
in both hands and began to labour among his flock,
preaching, teaching and administering the Sacraments
without any remuneration or reward. All he asked was
food and a bed to sleep on as he went from village to
village, for the priests of the penal days never had a
home from the day of their ordination until the day
they lost their heads or died a natural death. They
offered up the Mass in the ravines of the great mountains, the crevices of the hills, and in the caves along
the wild shores of the fierce Atlantic.

The history of the brave smugglers and the wonderful
priests of the penal times, if written, would be as interesting and as sad as the history of the Catacombs, and
the struggles and persecutions of the first Christians in
pagan Rome; yet there is no mention of how they kept
the lamp of faith burning brightly in Ireland in the penal
times mentioned in what is called Irish history. I have
read all the histories of Ireland published in English,
although one was enough, for from the first to the last,
they are a repetition of each other. They trot out the
battles of Clontarf and Aughrim, and the Siege of
Limerick, although there was not an old man or a cal-
lagh in West Mayo some sixty years ago but could tell
you about these battles from tradition with far more
eloquence and pathos than the writers of these histories.
I agree with Mrs. Green who says in her beautiful book,
The Making of Ireland, and Its Undoing, that a real
history of Ireland has never yet been written. After this
long digression, I will resume my Shanachus.

I have said that Dr. Owen Bawn had an only daughter,
Una, who married the famous smuggler, Shemus Fodda
O'Malley, of Carramore. They had seven children, five
sons and two daughters. Three of the sons when they
were grown went on board their father's great lugger in
Carramore. Shemus Fodda raised his two great prow lug
sails and his jib, for they never had a top sail, and yet
the craft never existed that could beat them to the wind
or overtake them when sailing with half-sheet. When all

was ready, Shemus Fodda drew in his hawsers and set
sail for Spain. Una and many of her relatives ascended
the great hill and sat down on its summit from which
they watched the lugger as she ran towards the southwest along the coast until she disappeared behind the
wild headland of Renvyle.

Shemus Fodda held on towards the southwest. When
he reached the terrible Slyne Head, he took in sheet,
and lay off towards the Blaskets, West of Kerry, and
when his sons came on deck the next morning, the
beautiful green hills of Erin were hidden from sight
below the horizon. Shemus Fodda had the blood of the
old sea kings of the Owls circulating in his veins, so he
held on his course and soon reached Spain. His three
sons disembarked and entered the hospitable halls of
the College of Salamanca, nor did Una O'Fergus see
their faces or hear their voices for seven long years.
At the end of that period, Shemus Fodda raised his sails
once more and sailed to Spain where his three sons
came on board the lugger as fully ordained priests,
Father Brian, Father John and Father James O'Malley.
Then Shemus set sail for Inisfail, and how well it could
be said and sung of them : —

> 'They came from a land beyond the sea,
> And now o'er the western main;
> Set sail in their good ship gallantly
> From the sunny land of Spain.
> O, where's the isle we have seen in dreams
> Our destined home or grave,
> Thus sang they as by the morning breeze,
> They swept the Atlantic wave.'

When the time drew near when the ship should arrive
off the coast of West Mayo, Una O'Fergus and her
relatives climbed to the summit of the hill which overhung their village, gazing wistfully all the day long
towards the southwest for their return. One morning
there was a strong northeast gale blowing down Clew
Bay when they reached the top of the great hill, and
they saw the lugger on the tack out to sea from Cromp
Island, near the mouth of the Killary, towards Clare

Island, and they were overjoyed. Still they became
uneasy, for the ship wore all her sails without a reef as
she scudded along almost leaning over on her beam-ends,
and the white spray was washing high across her bow.
When she reached Shivdilla, the most westerly point of
Clare Island, she put about and then she lay in on the
land tack towards the strand of Carramore.

Una and her friends hurried down the hill, and the
villagers ran towards the strand in order to welcome
the exiles to their native land. On she came, sometimes
raised high on the white crest of a wave, showing her
bows and much of her keel. The watchers trembled at
the sight, but Shemus Fodda was at the helm, and he
knew how to deal with the wind and waves; how to
ease the ship and yet keep her going. When he drew
near the strand, he shook out the wind, and the blocks
and pulleys sang out merrily as the halliards ran through
them. The sails were lowered, and the gallant craft
swung round to her moorings. A boat was lowered for
the landing, and soon the three young priests embraced
and kissed their mother. They blessed her as she knelt
beside the waves, and they blessed the kneeling crowd,
after which they all marched in procession to Shemus's
house to partake of a banquet, for Una had a beef
killed for the great occasion.

Soon afterwards the Archbishop of Tuam appointed
Father Brian as Parish Priest of Achill, and Father John
as Parish Priest of Ballinakill in northern Connemara,
and he sent Father James with him to be his curate.
Nothing is recorded of Father John or Father James in
tradition or in folklore, save that they served God and
their people faithfully, lived and died there, and lie
buried in one grave in the old graveyard of Ballinakill.

Father Brian, however, was the hero of the folklore
of the Western Owls during his life and for a generation
afterwards. When he was going to start by boat for
Achill to take up his duties, the weather became stormy,
so he determined to reach his goal by walking around
Clew Bay. He took hold of his huge oak camog which
was cut in the dark green wood of Collacoon, a stick
from which he was never parted until two hours before

he died in his sister's house in the village of Feenone, and this stick was all the wealth or property he ever had, for from the day he was ordained in Spain until the day he died, he never had a house or home and he never had a pound, a shilling or a farthing in his possession. All he asked was a bed and food, which he got willingly from the good people of Achill. He knelt and got his parents' blessing, bade farewell to Carramore, and set out on his journey.

When he reached Aughavale, Father Brian lingered to contemplate the then vast ruin which in its glory stretched down far into the meadows west of the road, a ruin which tradition says was not an Abbey but a great college where men were educated and ordained secular priests in ancient times. As Father Brian turned around to continue his journey, he saw coming towards him what he thought was a gorilla. This was no gorilla but a man, and I shall explain how he came to be in this condition.

Some six years before, there lived in Belclare near Aughavale a young married couple, and the husband was jealous of his wife, who was a pure, good woman. He was always scolding and beating her. One day all the villagers had to gather in order to save the good woman from his fury, for he was beating her and saying horrid things to her. The woman knelt and, raising her eyes to Heaven, she said, 'Musha, I leave it all to God Almighty.' As the man opened his mouth to abuse her, a devil jumped into his belly, as tradition puts it. The man went mad and ran about the country raging; for six years he never entered a house, never washed his face or clipped his hair or beard which became matted and entangled, and his toes became like the claws of wild animals as he went about arguing with some invisible thing.

'What is wrong with you, my poor man?' asked the grave young priest as the creature approached. 'There is a devil in my belly these six years,' shouted the man before he fell down in a fit of epilepsy. When the paroxysm exhausted itself, he lay on his back in the road, and the devil struck him dumb. Father Brian placed his walking stick against the fence, put his stole around his neck, opened his breviary and began to read. Then he stooped down and struck the man on the mouth with the end of his stole, saying, 'In God's name, speak.' 'Yes, Father,' said the poor man.

'Where do you feel the devil now?' the priest asked. 'He is in my left side near my heart,' was the reply. The priest struck him with the stole over the heart. 'Where do you feel him now?' he asked. 'I feel him in my thigh,' was the answer, so the priest struck him there. 'Where do you feel him now?' he asked for the third time. 'He is going out through the top of my great toe,' said the man, and the priest saw smoke coming out of the man's toe. 'In the name of God, stand before me,' commanded the priest, and the devil stood before him.

'It was you who caused this man to be jealous of his wife,' said the priest. 'It was,' replied the devil. 'Well,' said the priest, 'you will never trouble mortal man again, for I conjure and command you in the name of Our Lord and Saviour Jesus Christ to go down to hell, and to stand there on the crown of your head and never leave there until the end of time.' As the devil vanished, the priest said to the miserable looking man, 'Arise, and go to your parish priest, and repent, and return to your much-wronged wife.' The man did as he was ordered, and the couple lived together happily. This may seem a wild, strange story, but it happened in Belclare, as sure as I live. This was Father Brian's first encounter with the devil, but it was not his last.

When Father Brian was far beyond middle age, his mother died, and there was no way of sending him the news of her death, for it was winter and the weather was stormy. On the first night of the wake there was a great gathering of the peasantry, among them being a man named Paddy Malley of Bunowen, nicknamed Bryjun, who was supposed to have the loudest call of any man then alive in Ireland. Some of those at the wake proposed that Bryjun ascend Carramore hill and call down to Father Brian in Achill. Bryjun consented. He ascended the hill through the moonlight night, ob-

serving that a mild south wind was blowing. He stood
on the summit of the hill and shouted down in Irish,
'Father Brian O'Malley, come up here to Carramore, for
your mother, Una O'Fergus, is dead.' Three times he
gave this bellowing call across the waters of Clew Bay.
The people who accompanied him to the top of the hill
came down laughing at what a fool they had made of
him, and the incident was soon forgotten.

Just as the cock began to crow, a very tall, spare,
aging man with a great Roman nose walked into the
place where the wake was going on. He wore a coarse,
high felt hat, a black frieze cothamore, a black frieze
coat, vest and breeches, a strong pair of brogues, with a
pair of spatters by way of leggings, and he carried a
large oak walking stick. All the people at the wake
sprang up to salute Father Brian. 'Don't stir,' he said,
'for I'll not shake hands with anyone here until I first
shake hands with Bryjun, for it was he called me. I was
attending a call in Achill Beg, and when I left the house
of the sick person, I heard a call, then another, and then
a third, and I knew it was Bryjun calling me, for I
recognized his voice. I got into a canoe and crossed the
bay, nor did I bring a boatman with me.' So Una
O'Fergus had her three priests at her funeral after all,
and with much solemnity she was buried with her
husband in the old Abbey of Murrisk.

The tombstone of Una O'Fergus lies at the foot of the
old limestone altar, and the inscription on it asks for a
prayer for the soul of James O'Malley and his wife,
Winifred O'Fergus. In 1869 I raised that flag and I
buried the last of the old packmen of the West, Patrick
Aoidh Hugh O'Malley, of Shraugh, with them, for they
were his grandparents, and I dare say that flag will never
be lifted again, for that sept is almost extinct now in
Ireland. Almost beside that tombstone there is another
one also at the foot of the altar, which records the
death of another James O'Malley, the James O'Malley
who once owned the salt pans in Kilsallagh. Both these
James O'Malleys were first cousins. The reasons I have
gone into detail about them is that as time goes on
some of the stock who are in America may visit Ireland,

and what I have written may be of service to them in locating the tombs of their ancestors among the most ancient flags in the old, ruined Abbey of Murrisk.

The Wonderful World of Hugh O'Malley

When night set in, the company became hilarious and gradually the noise grew in volume until it was almost intolerable, so one of the grand old men of the West called for silence. 'Now,' he said, 'we have had much dancing and singing, so why not have some stories for variety's sake?' This proposal was received with applause. The old gentleman called on the last of the packmen for a story. As I scanned him closely, I could see that he was built on a large scale, for even in his old age he was at least six feet in stature. His forehead was high and dome-like, and on his left temple there was a large mole; his eyes were large and grey, and his nose was inclined to be aquiline. He drank as much whiskey as any man of his generation; he smoked tobacco and chewed it incessantly; he lost much blood in faction fights, and yet he lived to be one hundred and twelve years old. He was the cutest and keenest man I ever knew until a month before his death when insomnia set in, with the result that the loss of sleep caused his mind to wander and he imagined that all the men he knew in his youth and manhood were around him. He died in a state of innocence and second childhood. Such was Paurick Arida or Hugh O'Malley of Shraugh, the very last of that enterprising, intrepid race of men, the packmen of West Mayo.

'Musha,' said Hugh, a benevolent smile playing around the corners of his mouth, 'the sorra story I have, but I will give ye a piece of Shanachus, and as I proceed with it, if portions of it be dry and wearisome, some of it may interest you, for you will hear things you never heard before at any rate. I was born and bred in Carramore, which until the great famine was considered to be the largest village in Ireland, for it stretched from the great strand along the high road all the way to the mearing of Askalaun, and it also ran down the declivity towards Louisburgh until it met the stream which divides it from Cahir. Had a stranger lodged in a house there, he would not dare to leave it without a guide, for he would be unable to find the house on his return, so large was the village and so similar the houses in construction.

'In those days Carramore and Cahir belonged to an old gentleman named French who lived in the old feudal castle which stood on a rock in the lake of Carramore, a lake which was drained in 1847. Since the name of French is rare in West Mayo, I daresay Mr. French must have been a Galway man who was driven from his inheritance by the inhuman Cromwell and got this fodeen in exchange for it from the Commissioners of Athlone, for history states that they often did such things. However that be, Mr. French was cheated out of his holdings some years afterwards by a roguish attorney named Owen Cressagh O'Malley, of Belclare. This Owen Cressagh also cheated an old gentleman named Gibbons out of his castle and little estate in Kilmeena; the castle was called Cishlan Loff or Castle Laffey. The scoundrel, Owen Cressagh, also got possession of Clare Island by some law process or other. When Owen's son, Sir Samuel O'Malley, grew up and learned that his mother wasn't a lady, he shot her. She was the daughter of a Dublin feather merchant named Reilly. When Sir Samuel's sons grew up, one of them shot the other, and in his old age Sir Samuel lost all the estates his father had acquired by perjury and fraud.

'When I was just ten years old, on a certain day in springtime my father had a mehal or gang of men sowing potatoes. My mother had begun to prepare the men's dinner, and as she stood on the kitchen table to cut down some bacon hanging above, she suddenly fell off and died of heart failure. I ran to the field and told my father, and all the men ran to the house with much uproar and confusion. My mother was a McNamara from the far West. In the late evening her mother,

accompanied by her two other married daughters,
arrived, and their grief and lamentation were terrible
to witness. There was a roofless barn attached to our
dwelling, and when night set in the Banshee began to
wail in the ruined barn. My grandmother and my two
aunts got up from beside the corpse of my mother,
went out to the barn, sat down beside the Banshee and
began to wail with her. As the wail of the three women
arose on the night air and mingled with the wail of the
spirit, it was something weird to listen to, nor did they
cease this sound until the cocks began to crow.

'When the time of burial arrived, there was a long
consultation as to which of the two graveyards they
would bury her in, for there were two graveyards then
in the parish, namely, Dooya an thompal and Killeen,
for although Kilgeever gave its name to the parish, it
wasn't used as a cemetery until very recent times. Some
families buried their dead in the Abbey of Murrisk, but
none in Kilgeever in those days. The vast portion of the
peasantry in the far West believed that Dooya an
thompal and Killeen were the two most holy and
blessed spots in all Ireland on account of the traditions
handed down to them by their ancestors.

'In ancient times a vast green plain, or a beach rather,
stretched along the seashore from the village of Kina-
dooya to the mouth of the Killary, a distance of some
three or four miles, and tradition states that in summer
time this vast, beautiful plain was covered with bees
gathering honey from the white, wild clover blossoms.
High above the plain in a gorge on the side of the
stupendous Mweelrea mountain, there stood a little
stone church or oratory, dating back to the earliest
Christian times. This little church was roofed with stone
on the principle of the arch, like St. Dara's church off
the coast of Carna, or that of Ardfert in Kerry. Some
distance from the little church there stood four rude
stone crosses facing the four cardinal points, in consequence of which the gorge where the little church stood
was called by the peasantry "Maum na gress" or "cress",
the gorge of the crosses. There it stood, far removed
from any human habitation, some fifteen hundred feet

above the vast plain; there it had stood since the sixth century, but tradition had forgotten the name of its saintly founder.

'On a certain fine evening in summer time when the peasant girls from the numerous villages which lay at the foot of the great hill climbed towards the gorge in order to milk their cows which congregated there every evening, the little church stood there in solitary grandeur, but when the peasantry arose the next morning, the little church was standing on the green plain at the foot of the hill. There it stands like the House of Loretto, the wonder, the admiration and the pride of the natives who came in haste and amazement to gaze at the phenomenon, or miracle, rather, and the peasantry called the plain around the little church "Dooya an thompal", or the sandy beach of the church. This is the origin of that blessed graveyard, and surely it isn't to be wondered at that the peasantry of the far West wished to be buried there when their pilgrimage was finished in this vale of tears.

'Midway between the Killary and Louisburgh lies the vale of Cloonlara which cannot be surpassed for its charming pastoral scenery. It is surrounded on all sides by swelling uplands which shelter it from the prevalent storms of the wild Atlantic, and the verdant fields go down to a limpid stream which glides through the centre of the vale. When the river reaches the village of Cloonlara, it is sheltered from the prevalent storms. Here the villagers placed great square boulders at intervals across the shallow ford, across which they laid long lintels, thus forming it into a causeway for pedestrians, and in this way adding much to the embellishment and picturesqueness of the rural scenery. Amid such surroundings there once stood the venerable church of Killeen, and in the ground around it the peasantry of the central portion of the parish of Kilgeever were accustomed to bury their lamented dead.

'This church must have been a place of great sanctity on account of a privilege which it enjoyed, a privilege not enjoyed by any other church in Christendom, nor can I find anything in history to resemble it, save

among the Jews who caught hold of the horn of the
altar when in danger of their lives. The privilege, as
contained in tradition, is that no matter what crime a
person has been guilty of, even murder, if he escaped
and ran to the church of Killeen and placed one of his
fingers in the keyhole of the church door, he would be
let go free. Not a trace of this venerable church now
remains, and no one knows who the vandals are who
carried it away. In the graveyard there stands a Legaun
or pillar stone which is some seven or eight feet high.
This stone seems to be half Christian, half pagan.'

At this stage of his narrative the old packman, Hugh
O'Malley, rested and drained his glass before he resumed his shanachus. 'When my father was two years
a widower, he went down to Castle Laffey in Kilmeena
and married the daughter of the Gibbons whom Owen
Cressagh cheated out of his estate, and he brought her
back to Carramore. She was an angular old maid with
a pronounced aquiline nose, and when she looked at me
with her terrible, cold, steel-grey eyes, my heart sank
within me, for I knew she would soon comb my hair
with the tongs or the blackthorn, and from the day
she entered the house, I saw that my father only played
second fiddle. Some six months afterwards she took me
to the door and hit me on the posterior with a kick
which planted me on the dung heap, and she ordered
me out. Then I realized that I was an orphan and an
outcast.

'I knew an uncle in Cahir-na-Mart, but how to reach
him was the problem that confronted me, for in those
days there was no road from Cahir-na-Mart to the far
West. How then did the peasantry of the West reach
that town? All the principal villages were located along
the seashore, for a vast moor stretched westwards from
Kilsallagh to the vale of Cloonlara, a distance of at
least eight miles. This vast bog abounded with fens and
sloped down from the hills almost to the seashore and
was impassable even to pedestrians. So the peasantry
when going to Cahir-na-Mart or any other part of
Ireland followed the strand which stretched away from
the mouth of the Killary on to the Aughany West. Then

they traversed Aughany and Polgloss, and then had to
cross the rugged side of Carramore hill above the cliffs
which overhang the bay when they reached the great
strand of Carramore.

'It was then a vast green plain some thirty feet higher
than it is now, so they followed it and soon reached
Bunowen river which was then merely a rivulet, for in
modern times it is the drainage of the vast moor and its
reclamation which has increased its volume. They
forded the river at a spot where now stands an old ruin
called Lundy's Lodge. This ford was then almost as
important in its own way as the ford of Athlone was
in the old times, for it was thronged day and night by
pedestrians, horsemen and horses carrying heavy bur-
dens, and it was called "Augha na goppal", or the ford
of the horses. Once this ford was crossed, the people
followed the trail beneath the cliff of Bunowen and
traversed the great dourlin of paving stones before
climbing the smooth, big, swelling hill of Derrylahan,
descending it and passing through a townland called
Logadomba.

'Still they followed the trail along the cliffs of Legan
and soon they met the bright, smiling little village of
Legan which stood on the western slope of Old Head
hill. From here they turned East through Old Head's dark
wood at a place called "Leac-an-afrin" or the Mass flag
where the priest in penal times offered up Mass amid
the mountains. Soon the travellers met Old Head strand
which they followed and then that of Falduff; next they
climbed the little cliff and found themselves in Kilsallagh. Through Kilsallagh and Lecanvey they continued, and when they reached Murrisk they met the
Slighe or bridle road which the monarchs of Ireland
built from Tara to Croagh Patrick for the accommo-
dation of the hundreds of thousands of pilgrims who
visited the holy mountain annually. This road took
them to Cahir-na-Mart and the Midlands. I have given
all of these details about the route in order to show the
present generation of the West the road their ancestors had to follow when going eastward, and this
was the only highway we had in starting for Derry,

nor was there any other road from the West since the days of Parthalonus until comparatively modern times.

'Well, now, when I recovered from the effects of the kick which I received from the virago, I set my face to the East, determined like Jacob to reach my uncle at any cost. I was dressed as a female and had neither cap nor shoes, and I was just twelve years old. I ran along the great, green beach and passed over the Augha na goppal. Always I followed the beaten track, and I never ceased running until I reached Murrisk, where I sat down to rest in the shade of the historic Hawthorn of Murrisk, which is perhaps one of the most interesting trees in Europe. It is far more interesting than the one at Ardmach which carried on a conversation with St. Patrick, which was all it was capable of doing, while the Hawthorn of Murrisk was capable of depriving men of their lives.

'Midway between Westport and Louisburgh, a stream spanned by a bridge comes down through the deer park. Beside the bridge on the North side of the road there stood some forty years ago a little, thatched country cottage in which dwelt a brisk, hardy woman named Widow Machree who kept a sheebeen. At the East gable of this cottage there stood the famous Scahagh of Murrisk, the oldest and most terrible white thorn in Ireland. This bush was the terror of the O'Malley chieftains from the time when the Milesians first landed in Ireland, for if any chieftain of their name wronged a person, all that person had to do was to fast three days and nights, then go to the Murrisk hawthorn at midnight, dig three green sods at the East end of the bush, turn them down with the green side underneath, and at that very moment the chieftain fell dead. Strange to say, this hawthorn had no power over a peasant, whether he bore the name of O'Malley or some other name. Perhaps you will laugh and say, 'I wonder was the bush ever put to the test in modern times?' Indeed it was, and it did its work rapidly and effectively as will be seen in the illustration which follows.

'In the early part of the nineteenth century, there lived in the village of Cartoor, a place located on what

might be called the southern slope of Croagh Patrick, a
man named Owen O'Donnell, who was much-respected
and far-famed for his prowess and dexterity with the
blackthorn in faction fights. At the same time there
lived in Marino an old peninsular veteran named Major
O'Malley. On the pattern day of Murrisk in the year
1829 there was to be a pitched battle between the men
of the parish of Lecanvey and Murrisk, and the men of
the West, that is, of the parish of Kilgeever. There was
no quarrel or enmity between them, but they were going
to fight for glory.

'When the day came, both armies were drawn up in
the order of battle. The men of the West were tall of
stature, fair-skinned, fair-haired and freckled, and had
the physique of their ancestors, the De Dananns. The
men of the East had all the attributes of another race,
for they were broad and sturdy, dark-browed men,
descended from the Firbolgs, a hardy race who on many
a well-fought field delivered blow for blow, and who
frequently gave more than they received. The men of
the East were led by their impetuous leader, Owen
O'Donnell of Cartoor, while the men of the West were
led by the veteran leader of the Galvanaghs, Leim Dhu
Nicholson of Bunowen. There they faced each other,
ready to hazard their lives for the glory of winning a
victory. This kind of dangerous amusement was then
the order of the day.

'The two generals saluted each other according to the
courtesy of war. Then O'Donnell raised the cry high for
Murrisk, and Nicholson engaged him in deadly combat.
The action turned into a general engagement all along
the line so that the cliffs along the steep sides of the
blessed Reek echoed with the clashing of sticks and the
shrieks of frantic women whose fathers, husbands,
brothers and sweethearts were engaged in strife. Many
a brave man bit the dust and lay weltering in gore.
With Spartan courage, the Murrisk matrons took charge
of the ambulance arrangements, carrying the wounded
to Tom Polly's public house which the good man turned
into an impromptu hospital; the Murrisk young maidens
were the hospital nurses who bound up the wounds with

tender care. Then they gave each invalid a gill of Mrs. O'Malley's best fire water which was then considered to be the strongest stimulant on earth. This refreshment revived and invigorated the warriors who craved to be led back to battle. "Let stakes be placed in the ground," they said, "and tie us to them so that we may conquer or fall like our ancestors who perished on Ossory's plain." The young nurses chided their ardour and administered another gill of a liquid called poteen, with the result that the wounded men fell asleep, muttering and moaning as they slumbered.

'All this time the battle raged until the sun was sinking towards the West. The men of the East began to waver, for their general was wounded almost beyond recognition, his nose turned towards his left ear, and the loss of his right eye lending a sternness to his appearance. In good order the men of the East retired from the field, and although Nicholson was the master of the occasion, he was heard to exclaim, "Give me another victory like this one and I am undone."

'As O'Donnell and his men approached the gap which led from the field, they met Major O'Malley hurrying towards them, for he wished to review his youth by once again beholding a well-contested field. "Let me in !" cried the Major. "Not until we have passed out," said O'Donnell. The Major was a choleric old gentleman, and now he raised his great walking stick and struck at O'Donnell who anticipated him by striking a terrific blow on the Major's ear. The Major fell as if struck by a catapult, and his retainers carried him home. When the Major recovered, he evicted O'Donnell from his holdings. "Now, O'Donnell, I have my revenge," said the Major. "Yes," said the ruined peasant, "but it will be short-lived, for I will appeal to the white thorn of Murrisk."

'O'Donnell fasted for three days and nights, and at the third midnight he went to the bush, dug up the three green sods and turned the green side underneath. Before the sun rose across the hilltops, Major O'Malley was found stark dead in his bed. This event may have been a coincidence, but it is true as I live, and I know too that O'Donnell returned to his home and was never afterwards disturbed.'

Thulera, the Lazy Servant

Paurick Arida or Hugh O'Malley of Shraugh, the last of the packmen of West Mayo, smiled at the company, his large, grey eyes twinkling as he finished the last of the glass of punch and resumed shanachus. 'Well,' said he, 'when I had rested some time in the shade of the Hawthorn of Murrisk, I arose refreshed and resumed the journey towards the home of my uncle in Cahir-na-Mart. When I reached the field of Annagh, I lingered there to examine the graves of the pagan king of Killadangan and his lazy servant Thulera, and the graves of the unfortunate twin sons of William O'Malley. On the shore of the creek of Murrisk, I examined the boulder on which they sharpened their swords and tested their temper before they slew each other, those sons of O'Malley. The boulder is much worn by the friction of the swords which were sharpened there, and the two cuts made by the twin sons as they tested the temper of their sharpened steel are clearly to be seen on the rock to this day.

'What astonishes me most is that the name of the great pagan king is forgotten and buried in oblivion, while the name of his worthless servant is on every peasant's son even to this day, for if a man has a lazy son or a servant, when rebuking them in anger he will cry out, "Ah, you lazy vagabond, 'tis depending on Thulera to be depending on you !" In years gone by, often have I heard an angry parent scolding his idle son in this manner : "Ah, you lazy vagabond, when you were a little child nothing would keep you from running every night visiting to Tom Grady's, listening to all the backaghs who used to get lodgings in that establishment, telling about Fin McCool, Ossin, Diarmuid and Grainne, Cuchulain and Gaul McMorna, and telling about the pooka, the Banshee, and the old buck with the horns. Now, when you are fully grown and able to work, nothing will do you but this reading about Potiphar's wife, Helen of Troy, Calypso, Cleopatra, Catherine of Russia, Queen Bess of England, and that other vagabond of a woman, Dervargil of Ireland, bad luck to them. Faith," the father would say, "I wouldn't wonder but you are trying to be coortin', but no, you ugly villain, there is not to be found this day the girleen who would let you put your come-hither on her."

'It was this sort of scolding which handed down Thulera to posterity while his master was never mentioned. All that tradition knows about him is that his brother was Queen Maeve's first husband, and I dare say that tradition may be true, for any person who reads that wonderful story, "Táin Bó Cuailgne", can see that Maeve's first husband was a Murrisk man. The pagan king's palace was a white, wattled edifice which stood in the dark green woods of Killadangan; through a vista between the great oaks and pine trees it commanded a glorious view of the estuary of Clew Bay and its hundreds of fairy islands, while on the northern shore could be seen the cone-shaped hills of Tieranar and the great, dark mountains of Tirawly.

'High above Clew Bay there stood the Sinai of Ireland, the ever-beautiful Croagh Patrick. There it stood, the darling mountain, the pride, the joy, and the glory of the Connacht peasant, and no matter where his lot is cast, whether famishing in Manitoba, or sweltering beneath the sun as he climbs some terrible skyscraper in New York, Chicago or San Francisco, with his hod on his shoulder, he sees with the eyes of his mind the great blue hill on the seashore, the hill on whose summit Patrick talked to the angels. Then the exile sighs and weeps, for alas ! he will never more see it, and as the tears run down his furrowed, sunburnt cheeks, they are caught up by angels who hand them in at the gates of heaven. When he goes to sleep after his terrible day of toil and danger, he revisits in his dreams the happy scenes of his childhood and boyhood, but when he awakens, alas ! he finds himself an exile.

'Such was the scenery which surrounded the white mansion of the King of Killadangan. He felt so proud of it that he imagined he was lord and master of sea and land, and he said that to Thulera, his servant, on a certain fine evening in summer time. "Oh, don't mind the sea," said Thulera. "But I do and will mind it," said his master, "for it shall and must obey me." "I am in doubt about it, your majesty," answered the servant. "Come down to the creek," said the king, "and I will convince you, for I am determined to test the matter once and for ever."

'The tide was out, so they took two chairs with them and some iska baha, and they placed the two chairs in the centre of the then dry channel, sat down and began drinking from great horns of the water of life. Each was armed, and the monarch surely was a sight worth seeing, clad as he was in gorgeous, regal robes; on his brow he wore his most precious diadem, and in his hand he held an ivory sceptre adorned and embellished with gold.

' "Thulera," said his master, "I fear I have chosen a bad comrade, for you have the reputation of being the laziest man in all Erin. What say you about how you are going to conduct yourself on this momentous occasion, for should the water disobey me, I am determined to punish its contumacy." "Should it be so rash as to resist and disobey your mandate," said the courtier, "I shall assist in repelling and chastising it, even unto death." "Very good," said the king, "brace yourself by partaking of a few horns of iska baha, for the flood tide has set in, and draw your sword, for the enemy shall not ambush or surprise us."

'Just then the flood tide began to hurry in around the little headland of Annagh, and the channel began to fill and the water approached the king's sandals. He raised his sceptre and bade the water be gone, but the inexorable element continued to advance and soon rose above his sandals. The monarch arose in fury. "Draw your sword, Thulera," he shouted, "for the enemy is determined to charge us full tilt," but to his call there was no response for Thulera was fast asleep in his chair, oblivious to all that was taking place around him.

'The monarch had to contend single-handed with the relentless element which continued to rise and envelop him, rising above his hips. But, since he came of a race which fought to the death, he struck the waters with his bright, flashing sword, sending spray into the air to glint in the summer sunshine. He tried all the devices known to sword craft, but it availed him nothing as the water rose above his shoulders. Then he called and besought Monanaun to call back the waters, but the outraged deity replied, "No, in your vanity and pride you have attempted to deprive me of my prerogative, and those who defy the gods shall pay with their lives for their temerity."

'The king sighed and prepared for the inevitable, but before he died he administered a final stroke to the waters before he fell back exhausted and expired. Thus ignobly perished the great King of Killadangan, the last and greatest of his dynasty, the noble, young monarch who assisted Fergus in punishing the faithless Conor for his perfidy towards the three heroic children of Usnach, for tradition declares that it was his hand that drove the brain ball into the forehead of the deceitful Conor McNessa. When the tide receded, the monarch lay on his back in the centre of the channel, his trusty sword still grasped in his hand, and beside him sat Thulera on his chair as if slumbering. Then the druids, the minstrels, the poets, the shanachies, and the rest of the people came and with pagan pomp and ceremony, they waked and lamented the king and the courtier for nine days and nights, and on the morning of the tenth day they buried them at sunrise in the field of Annagh.'

The Town of Westport

The old packman, Hugh O'Malley, was fatigued by the
narration of his lengthy series of tales, so he lay back
in the chair and rested. A fair, beautiful peasant girl
approached him, carrying a glass of punch in her hand,
and as was usual in those days when offering any
alcoholic drink, she kissed its brim with her red lips
and said, 'Your health, Mr. O'Malley,' placed the glass
before him, and gracefully retired. The old man tasted
the drink, cleared his throat, and resumed the narrative
of his travels.

'When I found myself in Killadangan, I determined to
visit the witch's cave, for I had often heard the old
people talking about the witch who lived in it in the
old times. She had the reputation of being the most
terrible collagh who had ever figured in song or story,
for she could transform herself into any beast or bird
in whose shape she wished to masquerade. What she
did and how she did it, I am not going to tell on this
occasion, because I have other subjects to deal with.

'After I had examined the exterior of the cave, I set
my face towards the East and followed the old Slighe
Fodda which ran through the region of the green, swelling hillocks, lying between Killadangan and Cahir-na-
Mart. I ran through Belclare, Aughavale, Carranalurgan
and Ardmore until I reached the great hill on whose
summit now stands that demoralizing institution, the
Westport Workhouse. There was then no demesne wall,
so I descended the northern slope and found myself in
the sraid balla of Cahir-na-Mart, which lay at the foot
of the hill along the southern bank of the river. I entered the home of my uncle, Owen O'Malley, who asked
who I was. When I told him, he embraced me, and
then he lifted up his voice and wept.

'I soon found that the little town consisted of a long
street of thatched houses joined together; this street ran
westward from where there now stands the ruins of
the old Protestant Church until it reaches the present
Quay of Westport. It was a seaport, for the tide filled

the creek twice a day, and it was the principal rendezvous in the West for smugglers, fishermen and packmen. While I lived there, I often saw George Robert
Fitzgerald taking away cargoes of smuggled wine, brandy, rum, and leaf tobacco. The Brownes were looking
on, but they dare not interfere, for Fitzgerald only
wanted an excuse to shoot them. Later on, the Brownes
put a barrier across the creek, turning it into a stagnant
pool, and this act gave the death blow to the thriving
little Celtic village.

'Westport was a soft, easy spot to live in, for the
moorland was all around it, and the turf banks lay
beyond the river where there now stands that boxlike
structure, the so-called Castle of Westport. The ground
on which the new town is built was also moorland,
which abounded in blind, mossy pools, one of which
remains to this day and is called pool-a-cappal, because
an Augh Iska or lake horse used to rise out of it and
graze on its banks, but when the people approached it
plunged in again and disappeared in the bottomless
pool. There is a prophecy as old as the hills which pre-
dicts that sooner or later the pool-a-cappal will inundate
and destroy the town of Westport.

'When Browne compelled the inhabitants of the old
town to build the new one, he paved all the streets of
the new town with large round stones which he took
from Inishlyre, but when this had been done, it was
found that no traffic could be carried on over these
stones. At that time, Browne had twenty or thirty yoke
of oxen ploughing the bogs every day, endeavouring to
reclaim and fertilize the demesne, so he put the oxen
on the streets of Westport and ploughed up the stones.
Then he had the great paving stones broken and he
macadamized the streets with them, just as they are at
present.

'During the eight years I lived with my uncle in
Cahir-na-Mart, a packman frequented the house, for my
aunt-in-law was his real aunt. He always had two horses
carrying his wares, and he was then aged about forty,
for he had been some twenty years a packman. He was
the famous Tom Lavelle who composed the once-

popular song, "The County Mayo". One day he asked
his aunt to give me some money, saying that he would
take me with him and teach me the business. "I was
speaking to his aunt in Dadreen and she has promised
me that she will give him a horse," he said. So my aunt,
who was very wealthy, handed him thirty gold guineas,
and the next day I bade farewell to old Cahir-na-Mart
and set out for Dadreen in the far West.'

The Murder of Boyce Egan

'Musha,' said the old packman, Hugh O'Malley, 'the
tale I am about to tell deals with two subjects which
most engross the youthful minds of the present generation, namely, love and murder. When I set out with
the famous Tom Lavelle to learn how to be a packman,
we went to Dadreen in the far West where we were
welcomed with open arms by my aunt and her husband,
William Egan. They were considered the wealthiest
peasant couple in either of the two Owls of the O'Malleys, for the word "barony" was never used in those
days, but only the terms Owl Eagther for Burrishoole
and Owl Oughter for Murrisk. The Egans had only two
in the family, both sons, and surely one of them was
the finest young man I have ever seen. He was named
Behalagh, or Boyce Egan. When he found I was going
to become a packman, he decided to go with us. Alas !
that was an evil choice he made, as time revealed.
    'We took a supply of stockings and set out for Derry
where we arrived safely. Lavelle took us to the merchant he always dealt with, a very wealthy gentleman
named McKenzie who had no family save a fully-grown
daughter who when she saw Boyce Egan, fell in love
with him, nor did she try to conceal her passion. He
repulsed her since she was a Protestant, and no man or
woman in the far West had ever yet married a Protestant. She then offered to become a Catholic, but her
father objected. The next time we reached Derry, she

offered to elope with him, but he wouldn't have her in that way. Her case was a sad one, for she loved him to distraction.

'When we returned home from Derry, the girl Lavelle was engaged to had married in his absence, so he fled the country and went off to Jamaica, so we were left without our guide and mentor, and we decided to give up the business. At that time there lived in the village of Cross a man named Jack Davitt, a packman. He came to us and induced us to go with him to Connemara to buy stockings, and in an evil hour we consented. When we were ready to start for Derry with him, a strange thing happened. A champion wrestler came to the parish and challenged any man in the parish to wrestle him, but if none could be found who was able to throw him, he placed the parish under a tribute, and he had to be given a certain sum of money before he departed. This sort of thing existed in Ireland since the earliest ages, almost down to our time. It was for vanquishing a champion of this sort with the sword that Tubor-na-Lung was created Lord Mayo, and it was for a similar deed that DeCourcey became Lord Kinsale, and also claimed the privilege of wearing his hat in the presence of royalty.

'Well, I wanted to see the wrestling, so I set out from Dadreen for Toureen where Mass was offered up on Sunday, for there was no church nearer in those days. When Mass was over, the strange bully from Roscommon sprang into a field in which there were many stunted trees. He stripped himself naked above the hips and challenged any man in the parish to wrestle him. Not one man responded to his call, and like another Goliath he began to revile and laugh them to scorn. I was leaning on a fence looking at him. His taunts so enraged me that I sprang into the field and alighted on some loose stones which caused me to twist my ankle. Still I ran towards him while he stood and laughed at me, but before he knew where he was I caught him by the left hip and right shoulder, and I lifted him as easily as I would a child. I swung him around, and in doing so I broke his thigh against a stunted ash tree.

The roar he gave could be heard a mile off, but in fact he was the weakest man I ever handled. There was much cheering, but it's little I heeded it, for my ankle was throbbing painfully.

'I had to rest for three weeks, and the two Jack Davitts and Boyce Egan set out for Derry without me. When they drew near Derry, old Davitt proposed they should take some food. The food which we carried with us will astonish the refined present-day people. It was called Busthaun, and this is the way it was made : when the women made a churning, they kneaded the fresh, unsalted butter and oatmeal together and then formed it into balls as large as footballs. We carried these balls with us on the journey. Our ancestors maintained it was the most substantial and wholesome food on earth, and I do believe it was. The two Davitts and Boyce Egan went into a field and old Davitt spread a cloth on the grass, and so they sat down to dinner. Each man drew his skean dhu, or Irish dagger, out of its scabbard on his hip, and began to help himself from the great ball of Busthaun.

'When they were almost finished eating, old Davitt gathered up a handful of crumbs and with all his strength cast them into the eyes of Boyce Egan, blinding him. Then he drove his skean dhu to the hilt into his heart. Boyce, who was one of the strongest young men in Connacht, caught old Davitt, smashed him with his fist and knelt on his breast. Just as Boyce was about to stab old Davitt, young Davitt came from behind and drove his skean dhu into Boyce's back. With the daggers of his murderers driven deep into his body, Boyce Egan died, a young man who was said to be the finest and most beautiful man in all Ireland.

'Old Davitt took off the murdered man's shoes with the silver buckles and put them on his own feet, and then he took all his money. The two Davitts placed the corpse in a dry drain which was arched over by briars, and they started for Derry, taking the dead man's horse and load with them. When they reached Derry, Miss McKenzie asked old Davitt, "Where is Boyce Egan, for I see you have his horse?" "He is not well," said Davitt, "so he asked me to take it along with me." "How is it I see you wearing his shoes with the silver buckles?" she asked. "My own were not the best, so he lent these to me," he said, "but he didn't forget sending you the two balls of yarn he promised you for the stockings." She seemed satisfied with his explanation. When the Davitts disposed of their goods they sold the dead man's horse on the way home, and when they reached there they circulated the news that Boyce Egan got married in Derry and remained there.

'About a month afterwards old Davitt asked me to go with him to Connemara to buy stockings. I consented because I longed to see my cousin and comrade, Boyce Egan. We crossed the Killary and were bound for the fair of Dooneen. Halfway between Tully and Letterfrack, he asked me into a field which was surrounded by whin bushes. I agreed, and as usual he took out the Busthaun, spread a cloth on the grass and drew his skean dhu, but somehow I felt uneasy, nor could I eat any of the food.

'I got up and walked towards the fence, and as I looked along the road we had come by, I saw three men coming towards me at a great pace. They had their sticks on their shoulders and their body coats thrown across them. When they drew near, I recognized them. Two of them were brothers named Durkan of Askalaun, and the other was a man of gigantic stature named O'Malley of Glankeen. All three were yeomen. "Where are you going in such haste?" I asked. "Didn't you hear?" they said. "What would I hear?" I replied. "Jack Davitt and his nephew killed your cousin, Boyce Egan, about six weeks ago near Derry, and we are looking for them." "Keep quiet," I replied. "Old Davitt is in the field here. I will go down and spring on him, and then you jump in to my assistance."

'I walked back into the field. "Who were you talking to?" asked old Davitt. "Three strangers like ourselves who are going to Dooneen," I replied. "Sit down, man, and take some food," he said. I pretended to do so, but I sprang upon him, caught his two wrists and raised his arms in the air. He fell back, and I placed my knees

on his breast. The three men rushed in to subdue him.
We took the skean dhu out of his hand, bound him with
ropes, and re-crossed the Killary with him. The yeomen
took him to Westport and handed him over to the
terrible Denis Browne, better known as Soap the Rope,
who forwarded him to Derry. He was tried there at the
next assizes and was later hanged on the very spot
where he committed the murder. But no trace could be
found of his accomplice, the nephew.

'About six months afterwards, some children were
herding cows on the brow of a cliff in the village of
Dooaughtry when they saw small slates of shingle
being cast from the base of the cliff to skim upon the
smooth surface of the sea. Since they often did this
themselves, they knew it was some person who was
doing it. They told their parents who were aware that
there was a cave in the cliff and who guessed that
young Davitt was concealed there. They sent word to
Boyce Egan's relatives who gathered in great numbers.
They went in by boat and captured young Davitt in the
cave. He was handed over to Denis Browne, and was
afterwards hanged in Derry.

'The ends of justice were served, but Miss McKenzie
was inconsolable and pined for her dead love. She composed a lament for her lover which I used to sing in the
old days.' The company insisted that the old packman
sing it once more, so he sang them the lament of
Rebecca McKenzie for Boyce Egan :

> Oh, once I loved a noble youth
> Whose face was fair and bright to see,
> But since he died, in very truth
> This world is all a blank to me.
>
> For now he's gone, alas, from me
> Beyond that dark, mysterious bourne,
> Oh, never more his face I'll see,
> And I am left to weep and mourn.
>
> I'd climb with thee the mountains high,
> I'd brave with thee the raging main,

Nor would I even breathe a sigh
Lest that one sigh would cause thee pain.

I'd fly with thee to torrid climes,
I'd tread with thee their burning sands,
Thy voice to me were sweet as chimes
Of joy bells in my native land.

I'd live with thee in deserts bare,
Or in a rude cabin by the sea,
Nor would my heart feel pain or care
When thou wert there and I with thee.

Oh, leave me in a darksome cave
Where summer sunbeams never shine,
Nor fragrant flowers nor shrubs shall wave
Above this broken heart of mine.

But should we meet beyond the grave
In realms of everlasting bliss,
The only wish my heart doth crave
Is to lay upon thy brow one kiss.

Miss McKenzie pined away rapidly and died when the autumn leaves were falling, but before she died she became a Catholic, for she wished that no impediment should stand between herself and her beloved in the world beyond. Although the lovers were cruelly parted in this life by the daggers of the dastardly murderers, they sleep side by side in a fine tomb in the Catholic Cemetery of Derry.

Doonal Mergeach, the Bard of West Mayo

With much interest, mingled with regret, I have read the article by Professor O'Malley which appeared in a recent issue of *The Mayo News*. Last June I had the honour and pleasure of being introduced to him by a mutual friend, the learned, energetic Father John

O'Reilly, and was exceedingly charmed by the mild, unaffected, unassuming manner of the distinguished young gentleman. I was sorry to learn that his late visit to the land of the West in which I was born and bred hasn't been a success. Had he gone there some fifty years ago, believe me, he would have a different story to tell.

Surely the people of the West must have deteriorated terribly since I left, for when I left the West of Mayo some forty years ago, there were hundreds of old men and middle-aged men there who were brimful of songs and traditional story. Now it appears that these fine old Irish songs and interesting old legends are forgotten, and nothing remains save the remeshas of Shaun McNamara, Paddy na Stack O'Toole, and Leim Kirby of Askalaun. They were the last remnant of that terrible class of men who have figured conspicuously in ancient and modern Irish history and tradition, the satirical poetasters, who imagined they were poets. Their inspiration came from the belly, for if you gave them your sweetest bite or last morsel they would exalt you and place you on a high pedestal, but if you refused and didn't give it, they levelled you in the dust and set the world laughing at you. When I was a child in the great famine time, I saw these three satiric poets going about from door to door, and although I was then only seven years old, I could this day describe them, how they looked, and how they were clad. They received scant courtesy, so they perished and were swept away by the famine.

In the days of Michael Sweeney, there were two real Irish poets in Clare Island. One of them was a match for Sweeney in every way as a poet; his name was Shemus Dhu O'Kerrigan. The other Clare Island man was named Nicholas Doogan, but yet West Mayo never produced a real Irish bard, save one, whose name was Doonal M. McNamara, and it failed the professor or his favourite Shanachee and historian Pat Burke, of Devlin, to find out who Doonal was.

Doonal was the son of Brian McNamara who lived in the village of Caraniska, a townland some three miles west of Louisburgh, and old Brian was the richest man in his day in the parish of Kilgeever. When his son Doonal grew up, he was supposed to be the finest young man, not alone in Connacht but in all Ireland, and he was so fair-skinned and so freckled (for freckles at all times in Ireland were considered beautiful), that his friends from pride called him 'Doonal Mergeach', that is, Daniel the rusty.

There lived at the same time in Kilsallagh, a village some three miles East of Louisburgh, a man named James O'Malley. He was always called 'Shemus ui Thigue Bawn', that is, James, the son of white or fair Thady O'Malley. This James O'Malley owned great salt pans in Kilsallagh, and it was he who cut away that now worthless strip of land which runs along the cliff from the schoolhouse of Kilsallagh to Lecanvey, for it was there he had his turf banks. This man was considered the richest man of his time in the two Owls of the O'Malleys, and he had no children save a daughter then aged fourteen. Brian McNamara and James O'Malley put their heads together and made a match between Doonal and Rosheen O'Malley, who was in fact only a child. Doonal didn't want her at any cost, for he was paying his addresses, with much success, to a Miss Fergus, of Mullagh. The Fergus girls were famous for driving poets into exile.

At length Doonal had to give in to his father's wishes and get married to little Rosheen O'Malley, but his heart was in Miss Fergus's keeping. When he had been married about six months and was living with the O'Malleys, one night when James O'Malley and his wife were sleeping in the outshop of their kitchen, the daughter came down from the room carrying her clothes in her arms, for tradition states that she was so young she was unable to dress herself without assistance. 'Where are you going?' asked her mother. 'Faith,' said the daughter, 'I was afraid in the room by myself.' 'Where is Doonal?' said the mother. 'When ye go to bed,' replied the daughter, 'Doonal goes out every night through the window and doesn't return until the second round of cock-crow.'

The mother got up and dressed herself. 'Saddle one of the horses,' she said to one of the servant boys, and he did so. 'Now sit in the saddle,' she said to him, and he did so. The mother sat behind the boy on the horse. 'Now,' she said, 'drive on to Mullagh.' It wasn't far distant, and when they reached there, Mrs. O'Malley tapped at the door of Mr. Fergus. 'Are you there, Daniel?' she called. 'Yes, ma'am,' he replied. 'Well, if you are done there, come home,' she said. Doonal came out. 'I am very sorry to bring you out on such a journey,' he said to her, 'but I promise you while there is life in your body you will never have to take such a journey again.'

Then Doonal Mergeach set his face towards the South, and he never halted until he reached Crataito in County Clare, and he never returned to West Mayo. While at home he wasn't a poet, but when he became an exile it was then the Muses began to smile upon him. He took up the lyre and began to sing, or rather, to weep. When he composed a song, he transmitted it to some friends in the West, and his songs were considered masterpieces by the then clever men who dwelt in the West, and they were sung all over West Mayo for many generations. It grieves me to learn that Professor O'Malley met with only one of them for they were many. Often I heard my father and other men sing them, and when I left West Mayo, there was a man in Louisburgh called Thomaseen Meelan who used to sing them to perfection.

When Doonal's deserted wife grew to be a full woman, a man named O'Donnell from Ballacroy came with many of his clan at night by boat to Kilsallagh and took her away with them. This kind of thing was called 'foudagh', and it was quite common in those days. Afterwards, O'Donnell migrated from Ballacroy to Polgloss where some of his descendants lived until I left West Mayo. I dare say they are now extinct. When Professor O'Malley next calls to see his great Shanachee, Mr. Burke of Devlin, I hope he may be able to tell him who Doonal Mergeach was, but then the Professor might say it is some of Mr. Berry's fiction!

II: TALES OF CONNEMARA

At Grandy O'Donnell's Wake

It was evident that the old smuggler, George O'Malley, was in bad form for story telling, for the poor, homeless old seadog had walked all the way from his native place, Achill, to be present at Grandy O'Donnell's wake, but he pulled himself together and began his shanachus. 'Now,' said he, 'as the incidents I am about to relate took place in Connemara, a wild region, which few if any of the present company have ever visited, perhaps a description of it would not be out of place, although I would have you understand that this is applicable to Connemara as it was in 1798, and in a few remote portions of it down to a more recent time.

'Should you take a good map of Ireland, such as can be seen in the National Schools, and look at West Galway, you will see a bay depicted there named Kilkieran Bay, which runs straight to the North through the mountains to a place called Inver, where the present Earl Dudley has a sporting lodge on a small island in Lough Inver. From there a road runs to the North to a place named Shandilla, made famous by the late Major Lynam as being the spot where the famous Mick McQuaid kept a shop; this place is also now known as Maam Cross, and here there now stands a railway station on the line which connects Galway with Clifden. From this station a road runs north to Maam, then turns left through Maam Valley and Joyce Country to Leenane.

'When you reach there, you may imagine the coast line of the Killary to its mouth; all the vast region to the West of this imaginary line I have drawn is the great barony of Ballynahinch, or the vast territory of Connemara, the home of the exile and the outlaw in the old days. Of course, it is not all the wild region which our ancestors called Iarr Connaghta, but it is the impreg-

nable, inaccessible citadel of the wilds of Iarr Connaghta. Once you reached that region, you were as safe as if
you had taken refuge in the moon. There was no road
of any kind in this vast region, not even a beaten path.
There was no chapel in some of the parishes, no priest's
residence, no school of any kind, no post office, no
dispensary, no court of justice, no police barrack, for
there were no police until 1833; hence there was no
law, and everyone did as he pleased. The inhabitants
were split up into clans or factions, and the strongest
ruled the roost.

'All this vast region is almost totally occupied by
ranges of high mountains, notably the Banabola range
which is the pride and glory of West Connacht. These
mountains start up at Corrib in the East, run straight
westward towards the Atlantic, a distance of twenty-
four miles, but as they approach the great ocean, they,
like trees, begin to dwarf, as if stunted by the incessant
storms of the Atlantic. When they meet the sea, they
terminate in an amphitheatre of small, heather-clad,
picturesque hills, in the arena of which stands the neat,
modern town of Clifden.

'Between these ranges there are vast moors or
swamps, lakes and sluggish streams, tall bulrushes, and
a high, keen-cutting species of swampy sedge; woe to
the stranger who would try to pass through here without a guide ! The western coast line from the mouth of
the Killary to Slyne Head is thickly inhabited. When
you have rounded that dangerous headland, the coastline runs straight to the East to Galway, and this stretch
is thickly inhabited also, although the vast interior is
almost uninhabited, unexplored, unknown and un-
developed.

'How it was that the refugees found their way through
and penetrated this labyrinth of nature is truly astonishing. However, they came in hundreds, and were
received by the natives with open arms. The first thing
they did was to take native wives, for the Connemara
maidens of those days were easily wooed and won, and
within a generation or so the result of this union was
a race of mortals the most heterogeneous to be met

with in Western Europe. There was not a type to be seen among the Caucasian race but its prototype could be found in that strange, wild region, although later the great famine and emigration cleared them out.'

When the old man had finished his description of Connemara as it was in 1798 and long afterwards, one of the matrons of Cloonbawn came into the corpse-house to offer up a prayer for the departed. At that time there were many grand old matrons in the little town, but this one far surpassed them in hospitality, for she possessed a great share of what is termed the milk of human kindness. She was the noblest Roman of them all. As she arose from her knees, she looked around her and saw the old, homeless smuggler. 'Oh ! George O'Malley,' she said, 'did you come all the way from Achill to old Grandy O'Donnell's wake?' 'Yes, Mrs. McGirr, I did,' he replied. 'Musha, may God reward you !' she said. 'Come along, George, and have some refreshment.' He got up with alacrity and went with her, for I am quite sure he needed it, and yet I was sorry he left, for I longed to hear more about the wild region he had been describing. Alas, how short-sighted we poor mortals are and how ignorant of the future, for it is little I thought that night that one day I would dwell in that land and lay my bones in some lonely graveyard in which so many of my countrymen lie sleeping the calm, long sleep of, I hope, the just.

As the old man left the room, he promised he would return, but I thought there would be silence once more, but in this I was mistaken, for there were two strange mortals in attendance at the wake. One of them was the ugliest man I ever saw. He had a cast in both eyes, and both eyes were affected by cataracts. His cheeks were all puckered, and he had a terribly snub nose. He was knock-kneed, and his legs slanted out in such a way that his flat feet were set at least three feet apart. His occupation consisted in carrying the vestment box from one station to another for the priests at station times.

When the priests discarded their clothes, they gave them to this man, so he went about the town in a top silk clerical hat with a very broad brim, which it was said came from a bishop; he also wore a black clerical coat, vest and trousers, and he carried a huge, yellow walking stick. A priest he was to look at, but he lacked the Roman collar. All strangers saluted him at once, however. To do him justice, this distinction he never sought, but as the greeting was so kind, he returned it with the grace and dignity of a Cardinal, and in passing he raised his hand, uttering the familiar salutation, 'God bless you, my child.' Such was Paudeen Rory O'Toole in his day.

The other man was of a different type, tall and thin, with aquiline features. In those days the police could hand their old uniforms to any person who needed them and had cheek enough to wear them, so this man came in for a large share of them. He always went about the town tricked out in a policeman's rig, forage cap and all, and he sported a thin walking stick with a tassel dangling from it. He sang French and Italian songs, moroya, with the skill and pathos of a Caruso, for which he received many tips from strangers. Such was Gogie Ivers in his day.

'The old smuggler will get a good supper and a few bumpers of punch from Mrs. McGirr,' said Gogie. 'They will be of little use to him,' observed Paudeen. 'Why?' asked the other. 'Because if you put a tube from here to Loughnamucka, and put the one end of it in his mouth, if that lake was a lake of whiskey, he would soak it into him and drain it as dry as the floor of an oven,' said Paudeen. 'He was never fit to drink with old Paddy Malley of Shraugh,' said Gogie, 'for the wife of the man that's overboard here tonight, poor Nancy Mulloy, God be good to her, tried them at it. When the smuggler had taken twenty-two tumblers of punch, he fell asleep, so Paddy drank twenty-five, and then he took out his mare, Maura-nee-Ortha, and you would not notice that he had a drop taken.' 'He was a fool,' said O'Toole, 'for they say that mare was hard to ride, even by a sober man.' 'Not when you got in the saddle,' said Ivers. 'Anyhow, she was the best mare that ever figured West of the Shannon, for she never lost a race.'

'That was a queer name she had,' said Paudeen. 'It was a woman's name,' replied Ivers, 'for Maura-nee-Ortha means Mary O'Flaherty, and I'll tell you how she got the name. When Paddy Malley's son came home a priest from Portugal, he was sent as a Curate to the parish of Ballinakill in Connemara, and his father gave him a racer. He took lodgings in Tully at the mouth of the Killary, and in the same village there lived a woman named Maura-nee-Ortha, otherwise Mary Flaherty. One morning in the harvest time, her husband went out to his little field to reap corn, so after his wife had milked the cow, she went out to him and tied the six barths of corn he had cut. "Festy, agraw," says she, "go in to your breakfast, for I am going to the blessed well of Balla beyant Castlebar in the blessed county of Mayo, and when I return in the evening, with the help of God, I'll bind all you have cut while I am away."

'Then she took her ball of thread and her knitting pins and hurried off, knitting and humming to herself in order to shorten the road, moroya. It was not long until she reached Balla and gave her station. She arrived home quite early in the evening, and tied the corn her husband had cut while she was away. She milked the poor coween, and she had a fine pair of socks made, so she became famous as a walker. The young priest was very pleased, so he called the racer after her,' said Ivers.

'A man in Caraclagan had a mare,' said O'Toole, 'and his mare had a foal on Christmas night. "Take her down to the turf bank," said he to his sons, "and drown the foal in the boghole." They did as he desired, but the mare pulled the foal out again, and this took place three times, so they let the animal live. He was a blue colour and not much to look at. When he was three years old, horse races for a saddle and bridle were held in Toureen, for there was no Louisburgh in those days. One of the young McDonnells who owned him raced him there. He was in before any of the other horses were halfway home. "Who owns the brunnach?" asked old Tom Ruttledge of Ballyhip. "He belongs to me," said O'Donnell. So Tom Ruttledge bought her for six pounds. This horse won all the great races of his day in the British

Isles. He was taken to France and won all before him there, until he had to be cried down as being enchanted. This is no fiction, but a real fact.'

The Smuggler's Story

George O'Malley, the old smuggler from Achill, pulled his chair closer to the fire and prepared to entertain the company with the tale of his adventures in the wilds of Connemara. 'In the summer of 1810,' he said, 'I discharged a cargo of wine, rum, brandy and tobacco in the Killary. It did not take me long to do so, as I had agents on both sides of the bay who took charge of the cargo. Then I overhauled and tidied the lugger, for it was on her fast sailing and speed our lives depended. One evening as I leaned on the bulwarks watching the men who were scraping the ship's sides above the water line, I was admiring the western range of the Banabola mountains, for they were a wonderful sight decked out in their very best summer holiday vestments of purple, green and yellow. Each peak had on its white helmet which sparkled as the sun shone, and these mountains filled my mind with visions of giants who were determined to repel any invasion from the West. I have mentioned the western range, for the Twelve Pins are divided into two ranges by the valley, or rather gorge, of Glaninagh. This gorge begins at Recess where the railway station stands now, and continues on to the Killary, a distance of fifteen miles.

'One half of this narrow gorge is occupied by the beautiful Lough Inagh, while the other half is one vast moor, which slopes gently down to the southern shore of the Killary, and as I looked along this moor I saw a man approaching from the South. He continued on his way and never halted until he stood on a little bluff which jutted into the bay, from which he called out and asked to be taken over. I did not wish to disturb the men who were working, so I got into a boat with

my face to the bow, for the distance was so short I did
not think it worth while to sit properly on the beam.
I paddled gently towards him. As I drew near, he stood
some fifty feet above me, with his outline cut clear
against the dark blue summer sky, and as he leaned
against a long gun, the stock of which rested on the
ground, he was surely a man of the grandest physique
I have ever seen, for he seemed to be over six feet in
height, broad-shouldered, narrow-hipped, and light-
limbed.

'"Did you call out and ask to be taken across the
bay?" I said. "Yes, if you please, sir," said he. I wheeled
the boat around and he stepped in on the stern sheet
and sat down on the locker. He took off his hat in order
to wipe the perspiration off his brow, and it was then
I had a real opportunity of looking at him. He was the
straightest, the grandest, the most extraordinary man I
ever saw. He seemed not to belong to the species I belonged to, for he was as strange to me as if he had fallen
from the planet Mars. He was dark-haired, and the portion of it which his hat covered lay smooth and shining
on his beautifully shaped head, while the portion of it
below his hat curled up in deep waves which were
astonishing to look at. In fact, he had as much hair as
would spoil twenty men, yet somehow it became him,
and adorned him far better than the diadem of an
Emperor. His every movement differed from the move-
ments of the race of men I had been accustomed to.

'"How far have you come today, sir?" I asked. "Just
thirty miles," said he, "straight south from a wild peninsula called Errisanagle, just opposite the dark blue
Isles of Aran, a rough, unfrequented swamp which was
never intended by nature as a home for man, and yet,
it is inhabited by a race of ferocious giants. In all that
journey from there to here I have not met or seen one
of my own species, nor have I trod on solid ground, for
the region I have passed through is one vast, monotonous, swampy wilderness where no sound ever breaks
the stillness of this horrid region, save the screams of
the startled herons."

'"You must be somewhat fatigued, please come on

board the lugger and have some refreshment," I said.
"Not until I know who the man is who invites me,"
said he. "Surely I am not so easily decoyed as that."
"Well, then, if the name of the one who invites you will
dispel your suspicions, my name is George O'Malley, the
last of the smugglers, who is very much at your service," I said. "And I am Brian McNamara, the last of
the Rapparees of the West, for whose head Denis
Browne, the tyrant, has offered a bag of British gold,"
he said. We embraced each other and went on board
the lugger.

   ' "Now," said he, "I shall remain as long as you wish
to keep me, for I have no home on this earth, save the
great cave of Benlethry, high up in the cliff of the great
mountain which looks down on the grand castle of the
Martins, once the stronghold of O'Flaherty of the battle
axes, the terror of the invader." We sat over our punch
until deep in the night, for I urged him to become a
smuggler and join me. "I would join you at once, but
there is a certain matter which I fear would prevent
me," he said. "Mention it," said I, "and we may find
some way out of it." "Oh," said he, "it is a private
matter which only concerns myself and another, so
there is no use in going into detail about it." We retired
for the night.

   'The next morning a young man came on board, the
son of one of my agents. "Roger, is there anything
wrong?" I asked. "No, sir," said he, "only we have a
Station in our house today, so my father sent me to ask
you to join the priests at dinner, and I hope that Brian
will accompany you." When we had taken some refreshment, we were landed in Derreennasliggan where
we set out briskly across the great moor which slopes
upwards from Killary to Lough Inagh. We soon reached
the great, circular sheet of water, Lough Fee, which lies
midway between the Killary and the gap of Kylemore,
and as we trod along its banks the air was redolent of
honey from the heath bells on which we walked,
mingled with the scent of the water lily, the bog-bean,
and other aquatic flowers which grew along the shore.
Further on, we reached the miniature Chapel of Cear-

agh, the most diminutive Catholic Church in Ireland,
standing on a little hillock in the almost interminable
bog.

'Finally, we turned to the right and entered the pass
of Kylemore, and soon we were shaking hands with
hospitable old Roger Coyne of Powlacoppal. I had
known the old parish priest already, and now he introduced me to his two new curates. "This is Father
Edward Vaughan, son to Ned Vaughan, the celebrated
Westport smuggler," he said as he introduced me to a
very young, fair-haired priest. Of course I knew his
father who grew to be a very wealthy man in Westport,
for he was most successful as a smuggler, although he
was subjected to much annoyance by the Brownes. He
was married to a very fine woman named McCaffrey,
whose brother, Father Tom McCaffrey, died as Parish
Priest of Louisburgh in 1847 or 1848.

'When Ned Vaughan had sired nine children he left
Westport in his lugger, bound for Flushing, but he
never returned, and the people thought he was lost.
His wife and her brother, Father Tom, sent the oldest
boy to college, and after this boy was ordained, he was
sent on the mission to Ballinakill. After a year or so,
he emigrated to America, and the whole family went
with him. One day he was in his Confessional in a
church in Portland when an old, feeble man entered.
When he knelt, the priest felt a premonition of some
sort, so he asked the old man where he came from.
"From Ireland," said he. "What part?" asked the priest.
"From Westport, County Mayo," came the reply. "Have
you got a family?" "Yes, I have a wife and nine children." "Don't mind going to Confession tonight," said
the priest, "and I will accompany you home in order
to make their acquaintance, for I am also a Westport
man."

'The priest went to the home of the man, and there
he discovered that this was his emigrated parent, and
that the same number of male and female children he
had by his real wife, he had the same number by the
other woman, and the names were the same. The priest
told his mother the story, and when she confronted her

husband, the shock was so great that it killed old Ned Vaughan.

'The parish priest now introduced me to his other new curate. "This is Father Edward O'Malley, lately ordained in Lisbon, son of old Pat Malley of Shraugh, near Louisburgh," he said, as he introduced me to a very young priest with jet black hair, brown, lustrous eyes, and a long nose, inclined to be snub. This young priest became the darling of the peasantry as a result of an incident which I shall relate.

'When the road between Westport and Clifden was being built, there was a gang of men blasting in the then obscure village of Leenane, and in tamping a hole an explosion occurred, driving the man who held the drill high in the air. He came down in a sitting position, and there were no bones broken, nor had he any flesh wounds, but the cap of his skull was blown off from the two ears. He could talk and had his senses about him, and he began calling for the priest. The priest, however, was fourteen miles away, behind the great, high mountains of Kylemore and Salruck.

' "Don't be uneasy," said the poor, wounded man, "for I shall not die until I am anointed, for the Blessed Virgin Mary is standing here at my right hand. I see her with my eyes. Go for the young priest in Tully who has the mare." Then a man who was far-famed for his swiftness stripped off some of his clothes and his shoes, and he ran by short cuts best known to himself, through rugged hills, across vast moors and swamps, through tall bulrushes and keen-cutting wild mountain sedge. He breasted the great mountain and sprang from crag to crag with the sure-footed, elastic spring of the wild mountain goat.

'When he reached Tully, he quickly found the priest. "Hurry on, Father," he pleaded, "or you won't catch him alive." The priest quickly mounted his bright bay mare. "Now, Maura-nee-Ortha," said he, "you won many golden prizes for my father, for you have never been beaten yet in a race; gallop now and win this prize for God." Maura-nee-Ortha began to gallop. She raced from Tully to Letterfrack, then turned to the left through the wild pass of Kylemore, by the little church of Cearagh, and by the shores of the beautiful Lough Fee. Then she breasted the hill which leads to Clinncroff. She galloped through the evergreen valley and on to Derrynaclogh, and then swung round the Killary.

'When she got to Derrybeg, the people who were gathered around the wounded peasant sent up a great shout. "The priest, the priest is coming!" "Do not deceive me," said the poor fellow. "The priest is coming!" they shouted. "We hear Maura-nee-Ortha galloping; she is coming with the speed of the March wind." Sure enough, she was coming, but she seemed to be a white mare, for she was covered with foam, and her rider was white also, for he was covered with the horse's foam.

'When the priest alighted, all covered with mud and foam, a great shout went up. The priest took out his stole, kissed it and placed it around his neck, donning the sacred emblem which our ancestors believed helped him to remove mountains or conquer all the infernal legions, that emblem which has figured so conspicuously in all our ghost stories and our folklore. The priest put on his stole and anointed the wounded man, who with faltering voice said, "I leave you all my blessing, and God be with ye all for ever and ever." He lay back on the heath and died.

' "How long did she take to come, Father?" asked one of the bystanders. "She ran from the mouth of the Killary to Leenane in forty-eight minutes," said the priest. This was a distance of over fourteen miles. The news of this ride spread far and wide through the barony of Ballynahinch and became part of the folklore of the region, for there is nothing in the annals of horse-flesh to equal it.

'Turning to Brian, I said that if any of the Mayo rebels were present, I would appreciate his pointing them out. "Oh yes, I see five of them here," he said, "and they're seated together. Do you see that very tall, long-visaged man who is terribly pock-marked? That is Father Myles Prendergast, an Augustinian Friar from the old Abbey of Murrisk. When the French landed in

Killala, Myles and another Friar named Father Michael Gannon fled from the old Abbey and joined them. Father Mick, as he was called by the peasantry, put on the uniform of a French officer, but Father Myles, who was carefree, did not put on a uniform. When the French became prisoners of war in Ballinamuck, Father Mick passed off as a French officer, and afterwards rose to be a general in Napoleon's army, while Father Myles fled to Connemara, where he lives by playing on the bagpipes at all social gatherings." [He lived to a great age, and was stone-blind for many years before his death.]

' "The strong looking, fair-haired man sitting next to Father Myles is Jimmy McGreal of Ballyhip, near Louisburgh. He led the rebels against the redcoats at the battle of Collicoon, a townland near Louisburgh. The redcoats capitulated, so the rebels took their guns and shoes, and they returned quite crestfallen to Westport. Ever since, McGreal must be called Captain McGreal. He supports himself by training gun dogs for the squireens along the sea coast.

' "The pale-faced man with the watery eyes and long, thin nose is the loquacious, frivolous Affy Gibbons of Westport, who is a capital poet. He is the Poet Laureate of the same squireens. The young man next to him is one of the Jordans of Rosslevin, who was intended for the Church, but became a rebel. He is the tutor of the children of some squireens. [He was pardoned some years later, but was shot by Father Myles Prendergast, who suspected he was going to turn informer.] The man who sits next to him with the aquiline nose and the great blue scar on his brow, who is blind in one eye, is Jimmy Malley of Bunowen, who is always known by the nickname of "Go-go". He is a born soldier, and the bravest and best man I have met among the rebels.

' "When the French laid down their arms in Ballinamuck, the British soldiers were let loose on the almost unarmed rebels who were butchered in hundreds. Those who had pikes fought bravely. As I looked around me, I saw a dragoon bearing down, sword in hand, on Go-go, who held a pike. He had nowhere to fly, so he knelt on one knee and held his long pike before him. The dragoon missed him, for he didn't wish to come too near the pike, and his horse carried him some distance before he could recover himself. Then he came thundering on once more.

' "Go-go shortened his pike in order to tempt him, and when the dragoon drew near, the brave rebel shot out his pike and buried it in the stomach of the animal. As the horse was falling, taking his rider with him, the blow the trooper struck, although spent, struck the rebel on the forehead, gashing him from the eyebrow to the scalp. With the spring of a panther, Go-go arose and drove his pike to the handle into the vitals of the Saxon, who fell back weltering in his gore.

' "I hurried to Go-go's assistance and carried him to a little shrubbery nearby. I gathered some moss which I placed on the wound and tied tightly with my scarf. There he lay until night came, when I carried him towards a light I saw twinkling in the darkness. The light shone from the window of a peasant's cabin; the man bade us take shelter in his barn. There we remained for eight or nine days until the fever which raged through Go-go's body left him.

' "Finally, he was ready to travel, and we set our faces towards the West, but, alas, it was far away below the horizon. How I led him on, how I carried him across rugged hills, through soft, interminable morasses, fens and quagmires, and deep, sluggish streams, is known only to God and myself. At the end of three weeks we arrived at the foot of Benlethry, for our goal lay two thousand feet above us in the great cave near the summit, but this climb he was unable to achieve without more assistance. I left him to seek that aid, and when I reached the cave I found some forty refugees there. Four of them went down and carried him up the mountain, and in three weeks he was quite convalescent, but he had lost an eye from the inflammation of the wound on his forehead.

' "The man who sits next to Go-go is old Michael Sweeney, the poet, who composed 'The Wedding of Peggy O'Hara', 'The Ghost', and many other fine Irish songs. Beside Sweeney sits a small man dressed in a body coat of frieze, a frieze vest, and with knee-breeches over his stockings. He wears spatters, which are simply strong stockings without soles, the old Celtic legging. That man is Johnny Gibbons of Westport, the famous outlaw." [His inordinate passion for strong drink brought him afterwards to the gallows.]

'As we looked at the famous rebels of the West, Brian sang this verse softly in my ear :

> "They rose in dark and evil days
> To right their native land,
> They kindled here a living blaze,
> That nothing shall withstand.
> Alas that might
> Should conquer right,
> They rose and passed away,
> But true men,
> Like you men,
> Are plenty here today." '

The Prince of Lugatheriv

'Let me tell you about the events of that dinner at Roger Coyne's house near Kylemore on the day of the Station,' said George O'Malley, the old smuggler from Achill, as he finished a glass of punch and resumed his shanachus. 'The tables were set, the viands were placed before us in abundance, and we took our places. During the repast, I kept my eyes on my plate, but once the cloth was removed I looked to see who my neighbours were, and I became greatly interested in two females who sat facing me, for their dress and manner led me to believe that they were socially far above the people around them. One of them was in the prime of life. Her fair hair lay flat and thin on her smooth, ample brow. Her face was smooth and olive-tinged, and on one of her cheeks there was a mole out of which grew a wisp of fair hair.

'Beside her sat a girl aged about twenty-two, I judged, who was the strangest girl I had ever seen. Her hair, which was on the verge of whiteness, was the colour of a bunch of primroses you would see in May in the shrubbery, or in a little dell along the banks of a river. Her face was pale, but not with the paleness of delicacy, but with the alabaster shade peculiar to blonde women. Her eyes were closed, and the long, light auburn lashes caressed her smooth cheeks. To myself I said, "I wonder if this extraordinary girl is blind." My curiosity was soon satisfied when the old parish priest addressed her, saying, "Nula, my two new curates are considered the best singers among the priests of the Archdiocese; shall I get them to sing for you?" She opened her eyes and looked across at us, and as she did so, I felt myself shrivel and sink before her gaze. "Oh! do, Father, if you please," she said.

'Father Vaughan sang "The Cruagh", and Father Malley sang "The Coolin", not the one by Moore, but the original; old Michael Sweeney sang his own composition, "The Wedding of Peggy O'Hara". When Michael had finished, he said, "When a young man I was often at the blessed well of Kilgeever, and there I was often told that Brian McNamara and his two sisters were the three best singers in Ireland. I now call on him for a song."

' "Well, sure," said Brian, the last Rapparee of the West, "such as it is, you shall have it and welcome." Brian began to sing one of the grand old love songs of Connacht, songs to which I have listened enraptured as a boy, songs which shall never be sung again by the peasantry of Ireland, for, alas, their voices are now not Irish but English. Of course, these songs have been gathered and will be sung by people in over-cultured English tones. To put it another way, to the touch it may feel like Esau, but the voice of the singer is only the voice of Jacob. Brian's grand, sonorous voice swelled out and filled the room, and was wafted by the summer night air through the narrow valley between the great mountains. There was a rush of people towards the room, where they stood in astonishment, as if listening to Ossin who had returned from Tír na nOg.

'As I looked towards the fair girl I saw that she was sitting there with her large, hazel eyes wide open, her face all radiant, and her forehead lit up as if illuminated by some bright flame inside her head, and she seemed to be in an ecstasy. When Brian ceased singing, down went the eyelids, and there she sat as still as a statue fresh and fair from the chisel of Phidias.

'The evening drew to an end, the priests took their leave, and Brian and I started on our way to my ship in the Killary. When we were some distance from the Station house, I asked him if he knew the two females. "Oh, I have known them for years," he replied. "Who are they?" I asked. "The fair one, with the mole on her left cheek, is the daughter of a Scottish nobleman who perished on the scaffold for having taken sides with the worthless pretender. She is the wife of the Prince of Lugatheriv, a glen not far off from here, and the fair young girl who sat beside her is their only child. When I get on board I will tell you all about them."

'When we reached the ship I felt greatly fatigued as a result of not being accustomed to travelling through swamps and quagmires, for although my companion could skip over them without soiling his shoes, I would sink to the knees. Now I needed a little nourishment, and it occurred to me that a mild stimulant would be the best restorative, so I brewed a capital bowl of rum punch, which set me at peace with all mankind.

' "Sit down, Brian, dear," said I, "and quaff a couple of bumpers the short while we live, and let us live and enjoy it." "Oh, yes, with pleasure," said he, as he filled his tumbler and sat facing me.

'There he sat, this strange looking mortal whose enormous head of curly hair filled me with wonder, and I thought to myself that this must be how Absalom, the son of David, looked when he walked on earth. "Now, Brian, please tell me were you serious when you said there is here in Connemara a Prince of Lugatheriv?"

' "Why not?" asked he. "Haven't we in Connacht a Prince of Coolavin?" "Indeed, we have," said I.

' "Then why shouldn't we have a Prince of Lugatheriv?" he asked. "Surely there is nothing extraordinary
about it. The Prince of Lugatheriv is able to trace his
genealogy down from the earliest pagan times to the
present day, for his Pagan Firbolg ancestor, King Bola,
gave the name to the great range of mountains, the
Banabola, which means the gables of Bola. He fell at
the great battle of Moytirra and he is buried where the
Ballynahinch river discharges its water into Roundstone
Bay. The townland got its name in consequence of his
being buried there, and for hundreds of ages it was
called Tim Bola. It is located only a mile or so from
Ballynahinch Castle. A hundred times I have passed by
the great tumulus under which he lies buried."
' "What is the present Prince of Lugatheriv like?" I
asked.
' "He is a peasant man, but he still lives in the old
feudal Castle of his ancestors which will soon be a
heap of ruins, for it is greatly neglected and is hastening
to decay, the more's the pity, as there was only one
other like it in all Connacht. The other one belonged
to Quige na Builla, mad Thady O'Flaherty, the pirate;
it stood on a rock at the head of a little creek on the
southern coast, some two miles from Carna, and it was
called the Castle of Ard. The two castles resembled each
other, for they were built in the form of a horseshoe.
They looked like great Round Towers, but they were
encompassed by strong walls about fourteen feet high,
with a gallery or rampart all around the top.
' "In the Prince's Castle, which stands on a rock on
the western bank of Lough Inagh above which towers
the stupendous Ben Bawn, there are priceless treasures
in the shape of old curios, some of them at least 3,000
years old, which he would not exchange for the richest
Crown in Europe. In a room in his Castle he could show
you the Cotha More which his ancestor, King Bola, wore
at the battle of Moytirra. He could show you the
Caubeen stuffed with hay which the grand old monarch
wore on that fatal day. These great heirlooms the
Prince always wears when on the war-path.
' "He could show you the great war club of wild

mountain holly with which Bola severed the arm from
the shoulder of the Danann King, Nuagha, who ever
afterwards wore a silver arm and was named therefore
Airgiod Lamh. In a grand old wooden Mather of superior
workmanship, the Prince has stored some of the brain
balls which his glorious ancestors cast with much pre-
cision and fatal effect at their enemies. It was with one
of these over-shaped balls that one of my ancestors
struck Conor MacNessa and disabled him for life, the
false-hearted villain, and this missile at last caused his
death, which was well-deserved, in consequence of his
treachery towards the children of Usnach.

‘ "One of the most interesting souvenirs of Pagan times
is a wooden vessel which the Prince calls a goloon, which
is filled with three-cornered little pieces like pieces of
English slates. It was with these diabolical, magical
missiles that the Tuatha De Dananns annihilated the
Firbolgs, my ancestors, for the De Dananns were ma-
gicians, and by their art they were capable of raising
showers of hailstones which always came with the
north wind. Among the hailstones these three-cornered
pieces came and fell, and woe to the man or beast that
got even a touch of one.

‘ "The blow or touch was almost imperceptible, but
small as it was, the man or beast was a corpse before
the sun went down. These vile things were called sythes
by the ancients and were the terror of the peasantry of
Ireland even in Christian times. This was a nice mild
way of denuding Ireland of its people, and is practised
by the English of our time in another mild form, evic-
tion, emigration and the poor house. Of course, my
ancestors often rose against the Dananns, but it was of
no avail, for when our people were wounded by them,
they remained so, whereas when my ancestors wounded
the Dananns, they gathered a hundred white cows;
then they dug a pond, milked the cows into it, and
bathed in the milk. Then they arose from the milk bath,
quite healed of their wounds !"

‘This piece of shanachus aroused my curiosity to a
terrible pitch, so I said to him, "Brian, you must take
me to see the Prince and his Castle tomorrow."

' "Very good," said he, "I shall do so with pleasure."

' "Now," said I, "tell me all about his wife who, you say, is the daughter of a Scotch nobleman who died for the Stuarts."

' "The last effort the Scotch made, I think, was headed by the Earl of March assisted by Lord Lovat," Brian said. "Of course, this effort failed, and Lord Lovat was arrested and perished on the scaffold. His wife, who was far gone in pregnancy, fled from Scotland on board a Connemara smuggling vessel. The smuggler landed her in his native Ballyconree on the West coast, some three miles from where there now stands the town of Clifden. She told her story to the villagers who, with the hospitality for which they are proverbial, built her a rude cabin and furnished it with food and fuel. When the time came for her to be delivered and labour set in, there she was without means or money, without a fond mother to rush to her assistance in this most critical crisis of her life. She knelt in the rude cabin with great drops of perspiration brought on by the pangs of travail standing out on her noble brow and trickling down her emaciated, tear-stained, once beautiful cheeks. When the time came, she gave birth to twins, a male and a female, and then she swooned away as if she were dead.

' "There she lay on her rude stone pallet with her fatherless twins beside her. Can you realize the condition of this exile who was so luxuriously reared, the daughter of an Earl, the beloved and cherished wife of a Lord, whose gory head she saw raised aloft in the hands of the executioner as he cried out, 'Behold the head of a rebel !'

' "Many months went by after childbirth before she became convalescent, and then she determined to endeavour to support herself and her orphans by the labour of her hands. She became what the peasantry called a mantimaker. As time went on, her little ones began to toddle about, and soon she saw with dismay that her son, Simon Fraser, the heir of many titles, was blind. His hair was white; the peasantry of those days called such children Dall Bawns. The little girl was without blemish. The noble lady decided to counteract the evil to her son, so she began to teach the blind boy how to support himself against the day when she would be laid to rest for ever in some lonely graveyard in this strange land far away from the land of her childhood and youth. She took out the war-pipes of her dear, dead husband, and began to teach the blind boy how to play them, for she was a skilled musician.

' "Often through the long days, the noble lady would cease plying her needle in the art of the mantimaker, letting her beautifully shaped hands fall into her lap. Then would she cast her eyes towards her beloved Caledonia and sigh and weep, and the great, blue mountains of Scotland, the broad lakes, the rapid rivers, would appear before her. Then too would she see the form and face of her dead husband, and her beloved parents, and her brothers and sisters, and then the tears would fall once more.

' "Since she was a courageous as well as an educated lady, she taught her little girl to read and write English and French. Meanwhile she was much annoyed by the attentions of would-be suitors whom she repelled with scorn. How similar was her case to that of Sarah Curran!

> She is far from the land where her young hero
>   sleeps
> And lovers around her are sighing;
> But coldly she turns from their gaze and weeps,
> For her heart in his cold grave is lying.
> He had lived for his love, for his country he died,
> They were all that to life had entwined him,
> Nor soon shall the tears of his country be dried,
> Nor long shall his love stay behind him.

' "As her children began to grow up, Lady Lovat began to decline, and when they were fully able to support themselves, she took to her bed and soon died.

> O, make her grave where the moonbeams rest,
> Where they promise a glorious morrow,
> They will shine o'er her grave like a ray from
>   the West,
> From her own dear island of sorrow.

' "At that time, all tailors went from house to house making the clothes of the peasantry, and the manti-makers worked in a similar manner. When her mother died, her daughter, Miss Fraser, began to go from village to village as a dress or mantimaker. She wandered on towards the distant, towering Banabola mountains, and was employed by the inhabitants who lived in the little hamlet of Lugatheriv. Here the young Prince met her, fell in love, and married her. He was a very rich man then. When the sister had left her mother's cabin, the blind boy began to go around through all the villages of his native barony, then and long afterwards. He was passionately fond of music, and he earned his living as a piper."

' "Now, Brian, please tell me all that you know about that fair girl, the Prince's daughter, who sat beside her lovely mother tonight at the Station dinner."

' "Not tonight," he replied with a sigh. "This much will I tell you, that I saved her life. I kept her from a horrid death, but her parents are unaware of this. On some other occasion I shall relate this tale to you." '

The Rescue of Nula O'Flaherty

'When the Rapparee, Brian McNamara, informed me that he had saved the life of the daughter of the Prince of Lugatheriv,' said old George O'Malley, the smuggler from Achill, 'I became very much interested and longed to learn how he did it. In daytime aboard the lugger, Brian observed the greatest reticence, but when night set in and he had partaken of the fourth tumbler of punch, he was the best after-dinner talker I had ever met. In fact, he would be brimming over with anecdotes and legendary lore, and he could be coaxed on to sharing it by the invigorating juice of the barley which makes the best punch in creation. In fact,' said the old smuggler, while his aged face lit up with a broad smile, 'if you get the genuine Iska Baha, there isn't a headache in ten gallons of it. After dinner one night on the ship moored in the Killary, I mixed a capital bowl of the genuine punch, for by this time I knew it was Brian's favourite beverage, and I found that it would make him loquacious.

' "That's capital stuff," he said, after he had tasted a glass. "Is it strong enough?" I asked. "If not, I shall throw in another weesha cropper." "Oh, no, it's grand," he replied. "Well, then, help yourself, avick; don't spare it, for, thank God, there is more corn in Egypt," I said.

'Then I began to draw him out. "It's a wonder to me," I said, "that the fair young girl has not met some of the young Squireens along the seacoast trying to put their come-hither on her."

' "There is not a young fellow of note in the parish of Ballinakill or the parish of Ballinadoon and Omey but is after her," he said. "The Coneys, the Bodkins, the Darcys, the Corbets, the Slopers, and the poets and poetasters have all vied with each other in singing her praises. Affy Gibbons, the rebel poet, composed a song in her praise, but the peasantry only laughed at him, for he is too ponderous, affecting the style of Pope and Addison. It was not so with the song which Michael Sweeney composed in her honour, for it is sung both in Galway and Mayo even to this day. Sweeney, you know, was the Robert Burns of Connacht, and always composed in Irish and English, for he was a fair scholar, although he only learned in what is called a hedge school, which I hold are the best schools in the world.

' "The peasantry of Sweeney's day who could read and write were far and away the best and cleverest men Ireland has produced since, or ever will produce again, and I shall prove it. It is true that they never learned English grammar, but I hold that too much polishing wears away a thing, rendering it almost worthless, and I hold that too much polishing also wears away the human mind and deprives it of much of its natural vigour. The hedge schoolboys hadn't a regular set of

school books, so they took with them to school every
sort of book they could lay hands on.

'"The hedge schoolmaster was not the sort of man
whom Carleton and Lever have lampooned, no such
thing; he was generally a well-informed stranger, the
scion perhaps of some noble family who had been dis-
inherited by Elizabeth, or by James the First, or by the
inhuman Cromwell. The school boys carried with them
to these masters Homer's *Iliad* and *Odyssey*, *Paradise
Lost* and *Paradise Regained*, the *History of Greece and
Rome*, the *Arabian Nights*, Thomas-a-Kempis, Dr. Gal-
lagher and Keating, the Old Testament, Sallust in English,
Ovid, Ward's *Cantos*, McGeoghegan's *History of Ireland*,
and a hundred and one other books. Where they all
came from is one of the things that now astonishes me,
for these books were in every peasant's cottage on the
little loft over the fireplace, along with the wool-cards,
the balls of yarn, and the spindles; there the books
rested, some without covers, and all of them stained
with smoke. When a boy had his *Odyssey* read, he
exchanged it with another chap for his *Iliad*, and so on.
They spent seven or eight years at this kind of work,
and got them off by heart, as we called it.

'"Each boy and girl had a favourite Grecian or
Roman hero; some admired Socrates, some Leonidas,
some Lycurgus, some Xenophon, and some Cincinnatus.
The girls were taught to admire Susanna, Judith, the
mother of the Machabees, Lucretia, and Virginia, while
we all admired Hannibal. Often we had refined boxing
matches, with each boy standing up for his favourite
hero. This business was conducted according to the
rules of the ring, for we had two seconds and a time-
keeper, whose business it was to see that one boy didn't
hit the other below the belt, or when he was down.

'"The children were also taught how to sit at table,
and how to handle a knife and fork. They were taught
to salute and respect the aged, and to bow and draw
their bob or forelock to all strangers; anyhow, the bob
got its own share of pulling, for, alas, we had no cap
to raise. When these ragged little boys, some wearing
trousers, some wearing flannel petticoats, or dresses

like females, left off going to school and began to handle
their spades, their minds were made. In fact, they had
the minds of fully-grown noble men and women, for,
to their credit, let it be said that some of the girls were
the cleverest in the schools.

' "These little boys and girls when they left school
were better informed than the fully grown men of the
present day. One of them knew more about the world
than all the National School boys in the parish if they
were all melted down and cast into one huge National
School boy of this day. It was in these hedge schools
that the Irish peasantry learned to be steadfast, honourable and truthful, and to have fortitude, so that when
the penal laws and the persecution set in, they thought
of the woman and her seven sons in the Bible, of Daniel
in the lion's den, and the fiery furnace, and they held
to the faith of their fathers like grim death, and won.
I wonder, if the penal laws and the persecution set in
now in this frivolous age with its threepenny novels,
novelettes, and penny horror tales, would we be able
to give such a good account of ourselves. Indeed, I
fear not.

' "It was in these hedge schools that the Four Masters
first learned to read and write. It was in these schools
that Dr. O'Higgins of Ardagh learned to be a grand
Bishop and a great patriot, and last, but not least, it
was in a hedge school that the Lion of the fold of
Juda, the illustrious John McHale of Tuam, first learned
to be a great prelate, a noble patriot, and a melodious
poet. And it was in one of these schools that old Michael
Sweeney, the peasant-poet, learned to compose in two
languages, and in later life to sing so simply and yet
so sweetly the charms of Nula O'Flaherty, the fair
daughter of the Prince of Lugatheriv."

'Brian sang the words then in his glorious voice :

"In Ballynahinch there lies
A maid of great surprise,
No beauty can exceed this damsel's,
The beams that from her eyes
Would dazzle all your sight,

> Like Phoebus of a summer's morning;
> She's fairer than the swan,
> She's milder than the lamb,
> She's beautiful, discreet and charming,
> And if she went to Rotterdam,
> I'd follow her by land,
> Sweet Murneen, Nagroga Bawna."

' "All of Sweeney's songs can be found in Hardiman's *Bardic Remains of Ireland*," said the Rapparee as he drained his sixth tumbler, and yet he was quite sober and in grand talking trim.

' "Now, Brian, dear," said I, "talking is dry work; help yourself again, avick, and tell me how you saved the life of this lovely girl."

'He filled his seventh tumbler and then began : "When we fled from Ballinamuck, we all made for the great cave of Benlethry, and there we almost starved. Besides, we knew that Dick Martin had a regiment of yeomen in Ballynahinch Castle, which lay beyond the lake at the foot of the mountains, so, you see, we were in a sad plight. When I lived in Mayo, I used to do a fair share of shooting, and I learned to shoot straight, for why should a man fire unless he is sure to kill the object he fires at, when the report of firearms could bring two or three spies and gamekeepers around? Never fire if you don't know how to kill.

' "Luckily, I had a gun, and I knew that the mountains abounded with wild goats; they were domestic ones at one time, and belonged to a hag who lived in one of the glens at the foot of Benbawn. The old hag was called Colagh na Gowar by the peasant; she had no family, so when she died the goats ran wild, for there were no relatives to claim them. Benbawn has many cliffs on whose terraces the goats were to be seen in hundreds, huge animals with long hair which swept the ground. When we were almost famished from hunger, I took out my gun, which was a snipe gun with a very small bore, true and accurate as a rifle.

' "I had a long distance to travel around by Eaur na Noran and along the brow of the great, dark mountain

Glankohin, and then I began to climb towards the cliff
which overhangs the wild woods of Derryclare and the
ever beautiful Lough Inagh. I cut the balls I used into
four pieces, as you would an orange, and then I tied
these pieces together with a thin, cotton thread before
loading the barrel, so that when the charge struck the
object fired at, the thread would burst, with the result
that there would be four wounds instead of one. On
my first day, I killed four goats. Some of the starving
outlaws followed me and took the corpses of the goats
to the cave; from that day forward we had plenty of
goat flesh.

' "One day as I was traversing a deep glen from which
arose a steep precipice, I heard the heart-rending cry of
a woman, and as I looked above me I saw a girl rushing
headlong down the craggy mountainside towards the
cliff. She was being pursued by an enormous buck goat.
When she reached the brow of the cliff, she sent up
another wail. The infuriated animal rose on his hind
legs to strike her, but in doing so, he exposed his vital
parts towards me, and I shot him through the heart so
that he fell with a great thud at my feet. He was the
largest animal of his species on earth, for when the
men came and broke him up, they found twelve stone
of tallow in him.

' "When the girl realized her position, she became
unnerved and sat down on the brow of the beetling
cliff and sent up another cry. Fearing that she would
plunge headlong into the glen below, I put down my
gun and began to climb towards her. It was a perilous
undertaking, but it had to be done, and I had learned
climbing in my youth on the most precipitous mountain
in Ireland, my own native, darling Mweelrea. When I
reached the girl, I put my left arm around her waist
and led her down the steep, slippery declivity with
great care.

' "At last we reached the glen where the girl sat
down on a boulder and looked up at me with her large,
hazel eyes. As I gazed at her, I thought that she was
surely the strangest girl I had ever seen, so tall and
young, and with unusual hair. "Sir," she said, "you have

saved my life twice over, and you are a wonderful brave man. I am greatly upset, so I am unable to express my gratitude sufficiently, but when I recover, I shall do so. Please tell me who you are."

' "I am one of the outlaws, one of the refugees dwelling in the cave of Benlethry," I replied. "Very well, I shall call to see you and thank you there," she said, "on the last Sunday in summer." "Why on that particular day?" I asked. "Do you see that great mountain beyond the lake?" she asked. "Yes, I do," said I. "On the South of that mountain, which overhangs Recess, there is a holy well some two thousand feet above sea level; it is called Tubber Patrick, St. Patrick's Well," she answered. "On the last Sunday in summer there is a pattern held there which is surely the greatest in Ireland, and my parents will be there on that day, so I will have an opportunity of calling to the cave." "Please tell me your name," I asked. "I am the daughter of the Prince of Lugatheriv," she said, as she arose and went down the mountain towards the old Castle."

'Then,' said the old smuggler, 'I asked the Rapparee if he had ever been at that pattern. "Oh yes," he replied, "I have been there often. Where it is held is called Maum Ean, or the gap or gorge of the birds, because the mountains are so high that the birds when migrating North or South must fly through this gap in the range of mountains. The pattern is held on Garland Sunday, which the peasants call Doomagh Crom Duff. It is the greatest gathering of people I ever saw, and the most heterogeneous. They come from far-off Partry, from the banks of the Corrib, from the Joyce Country and Maam, from Oughterard, Carraro, Rosmuck, Carna, Roundstone, Errisbeg, Errismore, and Ballinakill, the wildest people in creation.

' "They come on Saturday and spend the night in the open air dancing, singing, and drinking poteen. Next morning they give their station, as they term it, and then they amuse themselves by engaging in the most terrific faction fights I have ever seen. It is often that men go to this Pattern of Maum Ean in perfect health and vigour, without a blemish, in order to distinguish themselves; they spend the night as I have described, and on the next day return home maimed and disfigured for life, some having their skulls bashed in, some having lost an eye, and some having a broken nose or a broken arm or leg. They could be seen about four o'clock on that afternoon, many with their heads bound up in turban fashion with the small, woollen neck shawls of their wailing mothers, wives, or sisters, who were leading them tenderly and carefully down along the steep mountain side, all the while scolding and up-braiding them as they descended.

' "Now, Columb," they would say, "we often told you to keep away from the Pattern of Maum Ean, but you would not hear us. What will you do now that you have an eye lost?" "Oh," the man would reply, "what about the loss of an eye when I have my soul saved, for didn't I give my station at the blessed well at sun-rise, with the help of God and St. Patrick?" He would stumble for a moment in weakness and then continue, "I wish every poor sinner in Ireland were in the state of grace and perfection I am in at this moment, but, forear gare they aren't." Another woman would be saying to her darling son, "Now, Greeora, what will you do when your nose is gone, for Nappy Tolan won't marry you, but she will surely marry your rival, Dudley Cloherty." "I will marry no girl in Ireland until I have blood for blood, and I shall have it at the next fair of Ballynahinch, or in Roundstone on Saints Peter and Paul's Day," he would bellow.

'Have you seen any of these fights?' I asked Brian. "Oh, yes," he answered, "I have seen the great fights between the Joyces of Joyce Country and the Malleys of Maam, and on the same day the battle between the Kings of Errisbeg and the Mannions of Cashel. These were the two greatest fights of modern times. The Joyces challenged the Malleys to fight them in Mau-mean on Doomagh Crom Duff. The news spread far and wide, so there was a vast multitude of both sexes gathered on that day.

' "The Joyces were the largest men I have ever seen, that is, each of them had a body as large as a feather-bed, and when I looked at them, for I have a critical eye for matters of this sort, I knew they would be beaten, for they were too unwieldy; they lacked suppleness and vigour, the two most essential qualifications of fighting men. The O'Malleys were about the smallest men to be seen anywhere, but they had the dash and vigorous energy of men who are determined to conquer, and they succeeded, for the Joyces were about the worst men I have ever seen in a faction fight.

' "The Joyces drew up in the order of battle, but made no effort to assail their foes, so the intrepid O'Malleys began the attack, led on by a very small, neat, fair-haired man, who turned out to be the most expert man with a stick I ever saw. The Joyces went down before them like stooks of corn in a storm, and in ten or fifteen minutes there wasn't a man named Joyce but lay stretched out on the heather, while the O'Malleys stood over them, thrashing them as though they were dusting carpets.

' "Then the other fight began between the Kings of Errisbeg and the Mannions of Cashel. The Kings were great, stout men, but the Mannions were the tallest men, I dare say, in Connacht. This was surely the battle of the gods and giants, and they fought on until the shades of night separated them, nor was the fight decided on that day, for it was to be renewed at the next fair at Ballynahinch."

'Bedad, Brian,' said I, 'the Pattern of Maum Ean is a very dangerous spot.'

' "It is seldom any man went there who ever returned without a wound," he replied.

'And what did you do, Brian, dear,' I asked, 'when you saw that darling girl again on the Pattern Day, or did you ever see her at all?'

' "Musha," said Brian, stretching and yawning, "it's tired out I am entirely. That will keep to another day." '

The Tribute of King O'Toole

'On a calm evening when the western sun was sinking behind the great blue mountains,' said George O'Malley, the old smuggler, 'I brewed a bowl of strong barley punch that Brian liked so well, and after he had taken a few glasses, I said to the last Rapparee of the West, "I wonder does the wife of the Prince of Lugatheriv ever visit her mother's grave in Omey Island?"

' "I don't know that," he said, "but I know that I went there, not to see the woman's grave, but to see the graveyard which was the scene of a very historic battle." "Please tell me about it," I said.

' "Oh, I'll tell you with pleasure," said he. "Some two hundred years ago, Omey Island was ruled by a monarch named King O'Toole, a grand potentate, not the old fellow who owned the celebrated gander, but far and away a greater monarch. At this time the Chief King of Iar Connacht lived in the great feudal Castle of Aughna Noor, which stood on the bank of the Corrib, and whose walls are quite perfect even to this day, the greatest and grandest ruin I have ever seen. This chieftain was named Morragh-n-Thua, or of the hatchet, who held sway from the Corrib to the Atlantic. One day he sent envoys to King O'Toole demanding tribute.

' "When the envoys reached the palace of King O'Toole, the grand old king was preparing to have lunch; he was a single old gentleman who had never married, and consequently he did all the culinary work himself like all old bachelors. He was just baking forty large potatoes in the hot ashes and cinders; when they were thoroughly done, he took them out and carefully wiped them, then he scraped the crust with the Sheen Duff which hung from his girdle. He then took a deep wooden bowl or dish and put all the potatoes into it, save the skin, which, when I was a wee chap, we called the pluckie, and which our ancestors looked upon as a delicacy, and always served for dessert. When the King was ready, he took about half a pound of old crock butter, and melted and mingled it with the potatoes, mashing them up together. This savoury dish was called bruteen. Doctors aver that this sort of pudding causes wind on the stomach, so King O'Toole must have often ruffled the waters around Omey Island.

'"The King next opened the family chest and took out a noggin of goat's milk. He sat down in his straw sheetogue or arm-chair, placed the noggin on one knee, the dish on the other, and helped himself to a wee lunch. He never could tolerate having a table in the palace. While he was engaged in eating, two tall pigs stood facing him in the centre of the chamber, vociferously squealing, demanding a portion of the savoury dish. In the door there stood two large goats with their hind feet on the threshold, and their fore ones resting on the closed half-door; their large horns touched the lintel, and their venerable beards fell down over their breasts. There they stood, for all the world like two old withered Oriental astrologers contemplating the stars.

'"When the old monarch had finished his light repast, he arose with dignity, shook out and adjusted his regal robes and addressed the envoys who had been waiting all this time. 'Whence come ye?' he asked them. 'We have come from the great Castle of Aughna Noor,' said they. 'Why?' asked he. 'We came to demand tribute from you for our master, the great King Murragh O'Flaherty.' 'Return to your master,' said the monarch, 'and tell him to come for it himself, and if he comes to Omey, I shall give him the soundest thrashing he ever got in his life, the plunderin' villain.'

'"Then King O'Toole began to prepare for war, for well he knew Murragh would invade his dominion. He possessed no arms or weapons of any kind, so he gathered about a hundred cart loads of paving stones which he caused to be piled in lumps above high water mark along the strand. Then he visited his arsenal, which contained one old fire lock. It was once a flint one, but the lock and hammer were gone, and the barrel had fallen from the stock.

'"The King consulted his chief sharpshooter, Festy Folan. 'Look at that, Festy,' he said. 'Well, I see it,' answered Festy. 'Do you think it will do?' asked the

King. 'It will when I twine it,' said Festy. 'But where is the twine to come from when I have none?' asked the King, shaking his head. 'Oh, I'll get some twine,' answered the sharpshooter.

'"In the sand hills of Omey there grew a tall kind of wild grass which sends roots through the sand a hundred feet long. These roots are as fine and tough as twine, so Festy bound the old gun together with this rude substitute for twine. Then he called his assistant, Darby Cloherty. 'Go down to the rock which is above highwater mark on the strand and build a small fire beside it,' he said. You can see that King O'Toole was determined not to be caught napping by the invader; in fact, he was thoroughly equipped for war.

'"When the envoys reached Aughna Noor, Murragh asked them if they had seen King O'Toole. 'We did,' they answered. 'Arra, musha, what sort is he?' the King demanded. 'Oh, he lives in great state,' said they. 'When we reached the palace, he was taking his lunch, and the table he used he would not sell or part with for all the gold you ever handled. While he was eating, there were two musicians standing facing him, playing the war pipes, and the music they made could be heard two miles away. In the door there stood two halbert men on guard, their bright spears touching the lintel, while their long beards covered their breasts.'

'"'By gob,' said Murragh, 'he must be a great fellow. What did he say when ye demanded tribute?' 'He said if he were near you he'd give you a sound thrashing,' replied the envoys. So Flaherty began to rage. 'I will drag himself and his subjects in chains and cast them into Cishlan na irka, in the lake shall I cast them, and let them starve,' said the King. He gathered his troops about him in order to start for the far West the next morning.

'"At this time Murragh had two grown daughters, one of whom was engaged to be married to the Earl of Clanrichard who was just then on a visit to Aughna Noor. Next morning Murragh set out for Omey Island accompanied by his two daughters, his prospective son-in-law, Clanrichard, and a vast army. In the afternoon they reached Claddagh Duff. When they looked towards Omey, they could see King O'Toole and his army drawn up along the shore. 'The savages haven't even a black thorn in their hands,' said Clanrichard. 'We shall have an easy victory,' said Murragh.

' "At full tide, a bay almost a mile wide separates Omey Island from Claddagh Duff on the mainland. At low water the channel is a vast strand stretching off towards the South. When the spring tides begin to flow, the flood water rushes in with terrific force and rapidity, but the inland invaders knew nothing about matters of this sort. The strand was almost covered with the flood tide when the invaders began to cross over.

' "All this time Festy Folan knelt beside the rock on the beach, his old gun laid on the rock; beside the rock his assistant had a fire in which he had the half of an old tongs, the end of which was a fierce red colour. 'Have you the iron rod?' said the gunner. 'I have,' answered the other. 'Now I am going to take aim,' said Festy, 'so when I put my left hand behind me, you will put the red iron on the pan in which there is some powder; do you understand?' 'I do,' he replied.

' "Festy took deliberate aim; he put his left hand behind him. There came the loud report of a firearm, and Murragh O'Flaherty of Aughna Noor fell out of the saddle, shot dead through the heart. With the rapidity of lightning, Festy charged again. 'Have you the iron in the fire?' he said. There was another loud report, and the Earl of Clanrichard of Punthuma Castle fell out of the saddle, shot dead also through the heart.

' "The horsemen turned and fled, with the water reaching up to their saddle girths. The infantry was then quite near the beach where they were cornered and assailed by King O'Toole and his army, who pelted them unmercifully with paving stones, killing them by the score. Then they looked behind them, but a broad bay lay between them and Claddagh Duff. There they stood between the devil and the deep sea, and they perished to a man.

' "Next morning there were six hundred corpses at high water mark on the strand of Omey Island. They were never buried until the wild sea birds tore them to pieces, and they rotted there. The stench was so great that the spot and the graveyard beside it were called 'Ola Breana' or stinking oil, a name it retains to this day. Thus fell ignobly Murragh the Great of Aughna Noor and his prospective son-in-law, Clanrichard, in a mean squabble, which was surely the greatest disaster recorded in traditional Irish history."

'Brian, Brian, musha,' I said, 'where on earth did you get all this shanachus?'

' "Tis a gift from the gods," said he. Then he tossed off a last tumbler of punch, took off his garments, retired to his bunk, and was soon fast asleep.'

The Battle of the Claddagh

'One evening when we were comfortably seated in the cabin of the lugger,' said the old smuggler, George O'Malley, 'we placed our steaming glasses before us, and then I asked Brian McNamara what he meant when he told me once that the Prince of Lugatheriv, when on the war-path, wore the Cothamore of his ancestors. "Surely," I said, "there is no war now going on in Connemara."

' "Not now," he replied, "but at election time there is always a war, and a terrible one it is too, between the Martins of Ballynahinch and the Frenches of Portacarran."

' "Are the Frenches able to stand up against Dick Martin?" I asked.

' "Caesar French is a top match for Dick Martin, or for George Robert Fitzgerald of Turlough, for he fought both of them. He is considered the best shot in Ireland," Brian said, "and none dare stand before him with a sword. Of course, neither of these men is worth a curse at close quarters in a faction fight, or trial of strength. The Prince of Lugatheriv would brain a hundred such men, for he stands six feet, ten inches in his stockings. In fact, were it not for the Prince, Dick Martin would never be able to stand up against the Frenches, for what Ney was to Napoleon, this man is to Martin, his right hand and the bravest of the brave. The peasantry of the hills look upon him as their hereditary chief, and four hundred mountaineers follow him to battle."

' "Have you seen any of these battles?" I asked.

' "Yes, I have seen the last one that was held, and surely that was the Waterloo of the Frenches," he replied. "When the last election was going to take place, both sides began to prepare months before the election day arrived, for this was to be the final struggle to see who would be supreme despot of West Galway. Both the Martins and the Frenches had estates in that terrible, wild region, and it was there that the best fighting men were to be had, those fair haired men of enormous stature. Two-thirds of them at least belonged to Martin, whilst most of French's followers came from the country around the Corrib.

' "French also had the sympathy of the inhabitants of the old city, for he claimed and prided himself as being one of the Tribes; consequently, the Claddagh fishermen, of whom there were nearly two thousand, always fought beneath his banner. In the Claddagh in those days there were six hundred boats, and each boat had a crew of three, so it was not a light job to face them. But it was their wives who did the most harm to Martin's followers. They came in hundreds, carrying skibs of filth and offal poised gracefully on their heads, and in the heat of action they cast their vile missiles in the eyes of Martin's followers, blinding them.

' "When Martin was prepared to start for Galway on the day of the election, he was placed in a position which caused him much mental disturbance, for his wife clung to him and would not let him go. She had a presentiment, she said, that he would never return to her alive. Of course, he had to go, so he set out, after embracing her; when he had gone, she swooned away and was carried to her chamber by her maids. Because Martin was too impulsive and too sanguine, he set out

without waiting for the Prince of Lugatheriv to join
him, and soon he, like all hasty men, found his mistake.
The Prince was quite a different kind of man; he knew
this would be a final effort, so he didn't leave until he
made certain he would win, determined as he was to
leave nothing to chance.

' "When all was ready, the Prince rushed down the
mountain towards the doomed city like Brennus and
his Gauls bursting down the Alps to reduce Rome to
ashes. Behind him ran four hundred fighting men, and
behind them came a hundred Amazons, led by big Anna
Connelly of Derryconly, the most ferocious and terrible
woman who has ever figured in West Connacht. Each
of these fierce women carried a new Connemara stock-
ing, in the sole of which there slumbered a paving stone
of some two pounds weight, a blow from which was
almost as fatal as a pebble cast from the sling of a
David.

' "When Dick Martin reached Galway, his men were
greatly fatigued after their march of forty miles, while
French's men were fresh. French attacked Martin's
forces as they entered the town and drove them back
towards Moycullen where they formed a cordon across
the road to hold them back. But this state did not last
too long, for the Prince was seen coming to their assistance. Martin's men sent up a great shout and opened
a passage for the Prince. On he came dressed out in his
full fighting rig, Cothamore and Caubeen, and in his
hand he carried his great club of wild mountain holly.

' "French's courage failed him, and he ran for dear
life towards the city, followed by his panic-stricken
followers. He ran until he reached a little square in the
centre of the city, where he rallied his disheartened
troops. This square is formed by the meeting of four
streets, namely Upper and Lower Cross Streets, High
Street and Quay, the latter of which runs down to the
broad, rapid river, across which there is an old wooden
bridge which connects the town with the Claddagh,
and it was across this bridge and along this street that
the fish wives always came to French's assistance, with
their baskets of filth. The battle raged in the square for

some time, with French casting many an anxious look towards the Claddagh, expecting the women to pour across the bridge. They did not fail him on this occasion, but when they entered Quay Street they saw a sight that they never forgot to their dying day.

' "They saw big Anna Connelly and her hundred demons come rushing at them, mowing them down by the scores, so that in a few moments Quay Street was strewn with wounded women, all besmeared and covered with the filth they intended for others. All who escaped from this treatment fled across the old bridge, nor did they look behind them until they reached their little homes in the Claddagh, where they bolted themselves securely. Then big Anna swung around through the fish market and entered Flood Street through the Spanish Parade. When French's followers saw those enraged Amazons approaching, a panic set in; they fled towards the green, and some ran to Claregalway, while others rushed towards Cranmore.

' "French retired to Portacarran, which became his St. Helena, and Flood Street, which was then the principal thoroughfare of Galway, was wrecked and in ruins. That evening Dick Martin was M.P. and Director of West Galway, and the Prince of Lugatheriv, his four hundred warriors and his hundred Amazons returned in triumph to the dark blue mountains." '

The Unwritten Law

'I could see that Brian had a story he wanted to tell me,' said George O'Malley, the smuggler from Achill, 'so I filled his glass once more, and encouraged him to loosen his golden tongue. "Brian, dear," said I, "you're a grand man with the shanachus, and you must have many stories of Connemara to tell me."

' "Well," said he, "as my name is Brian McNamara, and I come from a long and noble line, I have kept stored in my mind the legends of the people. There is a

tale about a proud, wronged man that I will give you
now. On the night when Dick Martin returned in
triumph to Ballynahinch after his election as M.P. for
Galway, he visualized the welcome he would receive
from his dear wife, how she would throw her arms
around his neck, kiss him and press him to her loving,
fond heart, a heart which had almost burst with sorrow
at his departure for Galway for the election battle.
These reflections caused him to hasten on his journey,
so that when he reached the Castle he had cause to cry
out like the Prince of Brefiny :

> "The valley lay smiling before me,
> When lately I left her behind,
> Yet I trembled and something hung o'er me
> That saddened the joy of my mind.
> I looked for the lamp that she told me
> Would shine when her hero returned,
> Though darkness began to enfold me,
> No lamp from the battlement burned.
> I flew to the chamber, 'twas lonely,
> As if the loved tenant lay dead;
> Ah ! would it were death, or death only !
> But no, the young false one had fled,
> And there hung the lute that might soften
> My very worst pains into bliss,
> While the hand that had waked it so often
> Now throbbed to a proud rival's kiss."

' "When Dick Martin reached the Castle, he found
that his faithless wife had eloped with another man,
and who that man was he did not know. All that he
could learn was that a ship sailed up Roundstone Bay
and cast anchor within a mile of the Castle in the little
Bay of Cloonisle, that Mrs. Martin was seen leaving the
Castle at midnight, that she was seen going on board
the ship, and that soon the ship set sail, and not another
trace was there of the lady of the Castle.

' "Dick Martin decided to travel through Europe in
search of the fleeing pair, disguised as an Oriental
diamond merchant; he took with him a faithful native

servant named Jimmy Pearl, who carried the pack of goods. Martin adopted a strict rule from which he never deviated; he would never display the rare trinkets save to the lady of the mansion which he visited. He set out on his travels, first searching every city of note and every great manor house in Ireland, without avail. Next he searched all England, Scotland and Wales, but not a clue could be found in any of these places.

' "Finally, he crossed over to France, determined to search Paris first. On the night he arrived there was a great ball at the palace of some nobleman to which all the nobility of Paris were invited, so Mr. Martin went there to watch the arrivals. This ball far excelled the great ball given years afterwards in Brussels, and ended far more tragically.

"There was a sound of revelry by night
And France's capital had gathered there
Her beauty and her chivalry, and bright
The lamps shone o'er fair women and brave men,
A thousand hearts beat happily, and when
Music arose with its voluptuous swell,"

Dick Martin rushed in among the throng of whirling dancers, pistol in hand, closely followed by his faithful servant, who carried a loaded pistol, also. There was a sharp crack, and the hostess, who was Martin's faithless wife, fell back, shot through the heart. The betrayed husband took the other pistol from his man and shot her seducer through the brain, and he also fell back, dead.

' "Of course, a panic set in, and all the guests stampeded towards the door. The old Dowagers, the Duchesses and the Countesses first ran, but it was their corpulency which brought about the terrible catastrophe which followed, for two of the Dowagers met in the doorway and got wedged together in such a manner as to prevent the guests from getting out of the room, nor could any human effort force them asunder. The melee began in earnest, for the old Dowagers tore each other to pieces. They tore off each other's false hair; they tore out each other's false eyes and teeth, tore off their coronets and crowns, while the paint on their wrinkled faces began to melt with the perspiration, making them hideous to look at.

' "Then the fair, almost naked debutantes made a rush for the door. Unable to force their way out, they became desperate and tore their scanty drapery to pieces. There they stood, as nude as Eve in the Garden of Eden, nor did they seem to be disconcerted by their appearance. During all this time, the gentlemen were not idle, for in seeking an outlet from the room, they tore off their willie-wagtail coats, their low-cut vests, the great white shirt-fronts; then the neat white trousers without any hose inside fell to the ground, and to complete the devastation, the well-kept imperials and well-waxed moustaches were plucked out and flung on the floor. There they stood, naked and shivering, knee-deep in the most valuable heap of clothing and gems which they trampled on as worthless possessions compared with one hour's freedom in the open air. There they stood, shivering and appalled before one brave man who had administered the unwritten law to two villains who had disgraced and dishonoured him, for whom he had searched for four long, weary years.

' "When the two Dowagers were at long last extricated from the door, they were stark dead and disfigured beyond recognition, for they scraped and tore at each other to the bitter end. They were gone to their eternal reward amid the evergreen bowers of the Elysian fields where, let us hope, they have become reconciled and are disporting themselves even to this day. Then there was a rush of naked people fleeing for their lives, leaving thousands of pounds worth of heirlooms ground into the dust behind them.

' "Mr. Martin walked deliberately to his hotel, nor was he ever questioned about the events of that night. Whether he married again, I don't know, but I know that when he died he left two grown, legitimate sons behind him, but whether they belonged to the first wife who fled from him, or to a second wife, I could not learn." '

The Martins of Ballynahinch

' "Is Ballynahinch a grand place?" I asked Brian Mc-Namara one night,' said the old smuggler from Achill. ' "Not at all," he answered. "When the first Martin, who was a trooper in Cromwell's army, invaded West Galway, there was no castle on the mainland, but Tigue na Builla O'Flaherty, the pirate, who lived in the Castle of Ard, near Carna, owned a castle which stood on a rock in Ballynahinch lake at the southern base of Ben-lethry. The walls of that castle are perfect to this day. Later on, when Dick Martin became chief ruler of the West, he used it as a prison, and any malefactor who was able to swim out of it got his liberty.

' "When the first Martin conquered the place, a fine Abbey stood on the banks of a deep salt water basin into which the Ballynahinch river discharges its water. This place is called Timbola, for it is here that old King Bola lies buried. In this fine Abbey there lived twenty-four Friars whom Martin took across the river to a little bluff or headland which juts out into the bay of Cloonisle, and he shot them all in the sight of their home. Since then, this bluff is called Curra na Brahir, or the headland of the Friars. Then Martin carried away the stones of the Abbey and built himself a castle with them on the mainland on the southern shore of the lake of Ballynahinch, an extensive, two-storey dwelling which enclosed a courtyard for drilling his murdering followers. Under this plain, low building there are many arches, and at each corner there stands a square tower, each of which has three levels. This castle stands in an old Irish wood, that is, a wood that was not planted by man; educated people call such a wood primeval, I think.

' "When Dick Martin died, his son reigned in his stead, a plain, uninteresting squire who is only remembered for three things: castle building, going into debt, and getting an Act of Parliament passed, which was then called Martin's Act. It is much in evidence nowadays, and is called the Cruelty to Animals Act. This

son turned the castle of his ancestors into stables and
built a new one on a bluff which overhangs the lake,
just where the river issues out of it on its way to the
sea. This castle is a long, plain, two-storey edifice,
having no artistic design or architectural embellishment
of any kind. It stands on the East corner of one of the
largest moors in West Connacht, surrounded by wild
Alpine country on every side. The son of Dick Martin
had a craze for castle building. He built another one
between Oughterard and the Corrib, which he presented
to the Government as a military barracks.

' "When he died, in 1846 or 1847, he left a vast estate
to his only child and heiress, but this estate was encum-
bered by a debt of three hundred thousand pounds. The
great famine set in, and there was no rent, so Miss
Martin, who was then married to a Mr. Goubell, fled
the country. She died in New York, a humble dress-
maker. The peasantry of Connemara who adored her,
called her Maria Martin. She was supposed to be the
finest, most accomplished and most beautiful girl in
Ireland. She always attracted praise, and when Daniel
O'Connell stopped in the castle the night before he
held his great meeting in Clifden, he christened her the
swan of Ballynahinch.

' "This lovely girl went about accompanied by fifteen
young peasant girls dressed in white, and as they walked
along they conversed in the native language, for Maria
Martin never spoke any language but Irish, save before
strangers. Her name was kept fresh and green in the
memory and on the tongues of the peasantry, but since
these grand peasants have now passed away, her
memory is now forgotten by those who have succeeded
them. I have often talked to scores of returned emigrants who had visited with Maria Martin, and who
had wept over her nameless grave in New York, and I
have never talked to one whose dark grey Celtic eyes
would not fill with tears as they described their sad
pilgrimage. Alas, it was in her case the innocent fourth
generation who suffered on account of the sins and
crimes of the first generation." '

Horrors of the Half-Way House

George O'Malley, the grand old smuggler from Achill, was in fine form that evening as he looked around at the waiting company, and took another glass of pure barley punch from kind old Mrs. McGirr. 'I have told you,' he said, 'that my friend, Brian McNamara, regaled me many an evening on my lugger on the Killary. One night he told me a tale which still haunts me on sleepless nights, and I will now tell it to you, but I pray that Saint Patrick himself will save you from the harm of recalling it when you are alone.

'This is the tale that Brian told. "From Ballynahinch Castle a vast moor stretches towards the South and West until it meets the wild Atlantic at Errismore, a distance of at least ten miles. It also stretches off towards the north-west from Timbola, at the head of Roundstone Bay, to Clifden, a distance of another ten miles. It is in the West corner of this vast moor that Marconi erected his wireless electric station, a truly wonderful invention. In 1798, and for long afterwards, there was no town either in Clifden or Roundstone, but two miles west of where Clifden now stands, as the traveller turns to Errismore, there stood a little Irish town or street called Ballinaboy, which consisted of about thirty low-walled, thatched cabins, fastened one to the other in a row. This town stood on the slope of a rugged hill, and had a bright, cheerful, southern aspect which commanded a grand view of the Alpine scenery of the picturesque region which stretched far away.

' "It was a place of much importance in the days of our simple ancestors, for there were four fairs held there annually, and without doubt, this truly Celtic street was for many generations the home of the Muses and of the gods of pleasure. It was the happy hunting ground of all the strange peddlers, pipers, fiddlers, hedge school masters, and quack doctors on earth. I believe they never slept by day or night, and nothing was heard there save the wild notes of the bagpipes, or the loud-toned voice of the Celtic singer; from one end of the year to the other there was dancing and singing, as well as the drinking of poteen, which was then sold at five-pence a pint. Not one stone remains now of that once gay place, and only the name of the townland is re-membered.

' "In those days all the packmen and strangers who wanted to visit the vast region towards the South near Roundstone Bay, Cashel, and far-off Carna, would tra-verse the great moor before they reached their goal. In the centre of the moor there was a hillock on which there stood a house, nor was there any other house near it within a radius of five miles. This was Derry-conly, the home of Anna More or Anna Connelly, who defeated the Claddagh fish wives in Dick Martin's elec-tion fight in Galway. Here she lived with her sister, Kathsha. In crossing the vast moor, this house was a landmark, for there was no road through the region in those days. In winter time, of course, many peddlers and others asked for lodging in this house, where they were received cheerfully.

' "But any person who ever entered that house never left it alive, for the inhabitants murdered them at mid-night. None saw the visitors coming, so there were no neighbours to criticize or question as to when they left in the morning, so the blackguards inside the house could murder with impunity. This terrible havoc con-tinued until the inhabitants of that house of horror were far advanced in years. One evening, a peddler asked for lodgings, and was, as usual, cheerfully re-ceived. He seemed to be wealthy, so they murdered him and found that he had a large sum in gold and silver. In dividing the money they quarrelled, and the two sisters and a brother named Columb (called More-na-Irka, big Columb with the horn, for he had a lump on his scalp as large as an inflated bladder) killed another brother, the arch murderer, Breen Dharag. Then they bound his corpse with straw ropes to which they attached heavy stones, and cast it into the lake, which lay just beside the gable.

' "The following summer, when the lake's level was lowered in hot weather, some little boys and girls were tending cattle when they saw something white at the lake's margin. They imagined it might be a large fish or a dead swan, so with the inquisitiveness of youth they went to investigate, and were horrified to see it was the corpse of a man. They hurried home to tell their parents, who went to Mr. Martin. Yeomen were sent out, and they were greatly astonished to find the corpse was that of Breen, the red murderer; they arrested Big Anna, Kathsha and Columb, who were taken to Galway, where they were hanged some time later.

' "The house stands there still, and is used as a herd's house. A fine road now runs beside it, connecting Clifden with Roundstone, and this house goes by the name of the half-way house, for it stands midway between the two towns. For six long years I have passed that terrible house once a week, in all kinds of weather, and home by it in the evening, a journey of fifty miles, and I never passed it but I thought of Anna More or Anna Connelly, her sister Kathsha, her brother Breen Dharag, and the other arch-fiend, Columb More-na-Irka, and the murderous deeds they committed there." '

A Journey Through the Wilds of Connemara

'One evening,' said the smuggler from Achill, 'I turned to Brian McNamara and said, "Brian, when first we met you said you had just come from a wild region which was far towards the South of Connemara, inhabited by a race of giants; were you serious or jesting on that occasion?" '

' "I was quite serious," he replied.

' "Please tell me about that wild country and its inhabitants," I asked.

' "Oh, yes, certainly I shall, but you will scarcely believe me because the story will resemble Gulliver's travels," he replied. "That region which I speak of is inhabited by two distinct races of mortals, one a dark, small race, and the other a fair-haired race of enormous stature; even up to this date there is scarcely any intercourse between them. The southern portion of the Barony of Ballynahinch is a mountainous peninsula, thrust out into the southern Atlantic, and it is almost an island.

' "It is bounded on the West by the Bay of Roundstone and the great salt water lough called Berter Boy Bay, one of Ireland's greatest, most secure, and most frequented havens for ships when Galway and Limerick carried on a great commerce with Continental nations in the old times. On the East it is bounded by the deep, picturesque bay of Kilkieran; on the North it is joined to the rest of Ireland by a narrow isthmus which extends from the head of Cashel Bay, in the West, to Inver at the head of Kilkieran Bay in the East, a distance of some four miles.

' "This isthmus is a morass and is considered one of the softest and most dangerous in Connacht, so dangerous that it brings woe to the unwary stranger who would attempt to pass over it without a guide. This wild peninsula, until the introduction of roads, was completely shut out from all communication with the rest of Ireland on the land side; in fact, it could be called the Tibet of Ireland. It was inaccessible from the land side, but the natives carried on a great traffic with Lower Thomond or the County Clare in turf and black seaweed by hookers, and so it was quite accessible to refugees from Munster who came there, and very undesirable aliens they were, too, for they brought with them in their train the secret society, Terryaltisnr, which almost ruined the simple peasantry.

' "Since the creation down to the time of the great famine of 1846, there was never a word of English spoken here, nor in fact until much later. When I visited this wild peninsula at the time of the Crimean War, there were only about a dozen persons among a population of 3,000 who could reply to me in English. And, although these people were Catholics, they retained all the manners and the customs of their pagan ancestors, and all their superstitions.

' "They believed firmly, and most of them believe it still, that none ever died here save the very aged, but that all the fully grown, all the youths and maidens, all the infants and children who died here are surely carried away by the good people or fairies. In fact, until the introduction of schools and roads, which are of recent date, they were as primitive as the Firbolgs or the De Dananns, who fought at Moytirra in Partry some 2,700 years ago. Their chief joy consisted in drinking their native Iska Baha or water of life, dancing and singing, for surely they excelled any other people in Ireland as singers of Irish love songs, for they were a very amorous people, may God forgive them.

' "When I set out on my travels towards the South, it was in the early days of June, the most glorious month of the year, and Nature seemed to be prepared to meet the eyes of a great connoisseur of all her works. The great mountains wore their newest garments, the trees had washed their foliage which sparkled with bright dewdrops, the mountain streams were stilled, but as I approached them, they began to run and prattle. In the midst of the heath bells the busy bees were humming, and the little birds were twittering in the brambles.

' "When I had left the Killary some six miles behind me, I beheld Lough Inagh with its numerous, wooded islands, and its strands of golden sands which sparkled in the sunshine, with the majestic Ben Bawn towering high above its western shore, while the Maam Turk mountains guarded the eastern shore. There they stood majestically like two giant sentinels guarding their darling lake, their magic mirror in which they had contemplated their rugged outlines since the time of creation.

' "It was a sight of surpassing grandeur, but I hurried on through the deserted village of Finisglin and the evergreen Cloon-na-Karthin or the oasis of the forge, and some three miles further on I cleared the gorge of Glaninagh and beheld a sight I have never since forgotten, for I was standing on the northern bank of a

vast lake which glittered beneath the rays of the summer sun. As I gazed down upon it with astonishment
and delight, I imagined that I had accidentally discovered the lost paradise of our unfortunate first
parents. There it lay in solitude and silence, well-
sheltered from the cutting winds of North and East by
the great mountains, while on the other sides its gently
sloping banks were embellished by wild woods in which
the Rowan tree and the evergreen holly predominated,
and from which the cuckoo's sweet call resounded.

' "Now," I cried in ecstasy, "I am surely the greatest
man in Europe, for although I am an explorer for only
half a day, I have discovered the long lost, much sought
for Garden of Eden, and I have placed Humbolt, Mungo
Parke, Livingstone and Stanley in the shade for ever.
Marconi will look insignificant in the future when
standing beside me." Then I set down the date of my
great discovery, and in order to make sure of identifying
the location in the future, I began to map it out
accurately. But, in looking towards the southwestern
bank, I beheld something which nearly killed me, for I
beheld a great village where I had thought all was wild
territory. "Ah, no!" I said, "it is only a mirage." I took
off my glasses and wiped them carefully, then replaced
them. Alas, it was not an optical illusion, but a palpable
fact.

' "There was the barking of dogs, the crowing of
cocks, the neighing of horses, the lowing of kine, the
bleating of sheep mingled with the milkmaid's song and
the joyous laughter of children at play wafted towards
me by the gentle wind across the placid waters. Then
I knew that I had been forestalled by some other dis-
coverer, and the shock was so terrific that I fell back
on the heather and swooned away. Some years later, a
gentleman named Sean Mahon, who I think was a
Westport man, saw this charming spot, so he set to
work and built a neat house on the southern shore of
the lake, since time immemorial named Gorramon, but
he called his place Glendalough, for there were two
lakes there.

' "Later, another gentleman named Hudsar passed this

way. Charmed by the scenery, he built in 1844 a plain, one storey cottage on a little platform on the northern side of the lake at the foot of Lissouter Hill, in which is located the great green marble quarry, one of the greatest in Europe, out of which has been taken many of the pillars which support and adorn the great new Cathedral of Westminster. This gentleman named his place Recess, but the name given to this spot since time immemorial was Shraugh Sallagh. It is on the site of this plain cottage that the present Railway Hotel now stands. Later, still another gentleman came along, a Mr. Meacreedy, and he also was charmed by the scenery, so he built a neat cottage with French windows on the eastern side of the lake. It was a raw, bleak spot in winter, but in summer it was grand beyond measure, for it commanded a full view of the whole lake and the sunset. When I recovered from my swoon, I arose and pulled myself together.

' "With much vigour and energy I faced towards the West, but soon I was confronted by a deep, dark, sluggish river, all overgrown with white and yellow water lilies. This terrible spot, which connects Recess lake with Lough Derryclare was then known as Beal Dhu Kora, which means the mouth of the black causeway, although there was no causeway, but only huge, uneven, slippery stepping stones placed there by Nature. As I went to investigate this terrible trap, I was appalled at seeing in the centre of the river beside one of the stepping stones, a young man drowned there, and his coarse Kilmarnock or Tam-o-Shanter lay floating on the water lilies beside him.

' "He lay on his right side, kept afloat by a great back load of willow and hazel brambles bound to him by a rope across his arm and breast. His mouth was open, and his grey eyes were wide open and seemed to be glaring at me. Had he carried his load on one shoulder as they do in Mayo, this terrible fate would not have befallen him, for his arms would be free, but the custom of the dead young man's country is to leave the 'crish' or hanger so long that they can insert the head in it; then the hanger is pulled down across the arms

and breast, and so if a man slips, he generally strangles.
I have in my time seen many deaths brought about in
this way. On the opposite bank of the river there sat a
great, blue-coloured Irish wolf-dog, whining and looking
at me with his great, brown, human-looking eyes as if
beseeching me to rescue his master, but this was out of
my power. I set my teeth and cleared the body with a
spring, and then I drew a long breath which was almost
a sigh, as men do who have escaped death by the skin
of the teeth.

' "There was no use in loitering, so I held on my
course along the western shore of the lake, and when I
climbed the bank I beheld another oval shaped body of
water; when I thought that I had reached the end of
this second lake, I found to my dismay that it was
joined to another one in the form of an hour-glass, or
like the arithmetical figure eight. The narrow spot
seemed to be shallow for I could see the granite pebbles
shining on the bottom, so I sounded it with my stick
as I waded through it and passed over.

' "Then I climbed a steep, narrow ravine all overgrown by a hazel brushwood, and skirted a fine cascade
which roared and tumbled into the lake below. Soon I
found myself in a great limestone village in the midst
of the wilderness surrounded by the grandest landscape.
I asked myself, 'Am I in Mexico, or in Peru, in the
capital of the Incas?' I was in neither, but I was in the
very centre of the wild, great parish of Ballynahincha.
I had arrived in the village of Gurramon, one of the
grandest in Connacht.

' "Soon I was standing at the door of John Thomas
MacJoyce, who kept what was then called a carman's
stage, and his son, Neddy John Thomas, as he was called,
one of the finest young men I ever saw, came to salute
me and welcome the homeless, footsore wanderer, the
friendless Mayo exile. Neddy Joyce brought me in and
introduced me to the middle-aged mother, the most
matronly and the grandest peasant woman I ever saw,
and to his sister, the most beautiful, brown haired,
brown eyed girl I ever beheld. She was only the daughter of a peasant,

'Yet England's proud Queen
Has less rank in her heart,
And less grace in her mien.'

' "The modest, pure peasant girl hastened to offer me
refreshments. 'Now,' said the mother, 'the first beverage
is the prerogative of this Irish matron. When the stranger arrived, I put down the skillet in order to make him
a possit. It is now just ready, so when he partakes of it
from the hands of the woman of the house, then it is
your turn to regale him.' A possit was fresh new milk
boiled up, and when almost at the point of boiling over,
a wee drop of thick milk would be cast into it with
much care and skill lest it would turn into whey or
curds. This drink preceded all others. Alas ! I fear this
fine old custom is now done away with in Ireland, for
surely Ireland is much changed.

' "The village stood on a slighe which could not be
called a road, for it was only a narrow, paved pathway
which wound around the hills from Roundstone Bay to
Galway. On the street or 'Kimeen' I counted at Mr.
Joyce's door fifty-eight Irish carts laden with herrings
on their way from Roundstone to Ballinrobe, and the
interior of Connacht. The village seemed to be one of
the largest and wealthiest in the province. This was not
to be wondered at, for it had unlimited pasturage in
hills and moorland, and it seemed to be the happiest
community on earth. As time went on, the great engi-
neer, Mr. Nimmo, began to construct the new road from
Galway to Clifden. When he reached the lake, he ran
the new road along the northern shore by Recess. This
changed away the traffic from the village, so that in
three or four years there was no trace of it or its once
happy,prosperous inhabitants. A thousand times since
then I have passed by this once happy but now deserted
spot, and I always ask myself how is it or why is it
that a million such once-happy villages with their
chaste, virtuous inhabitants have been obliterated in
Ireland, as if by the four winds of heaven, or by the
bright, flashing sword of some destroying angel, while
the great towns with their sensual inhabitants are left

prosperous.

' "When I had partaken of the viands which were so
lavishly set before me by the hospitable family, I set
out refreshed and found myself on a high table land
which was a vast moor stretching off westward towards
Athree, Ballinafad and Ballynahinch, and which swept
gently South, while high above to the East rose the wild
mountains of Lettershauna and Glantirkeen. After I had
traversed this wild prairie, I entered through a gap
between the hills the bright village of Glantirkeen surrounded on all sides, save the South, by heather-clad
hills. The valley is sheltered from the western winds by
the high, cone-shaped hill of Cashel, from whose base
it slopes gently down to a fine lake with many wooded
islands lying along the foot of the mountain. The bright
summer's sun shines in this sheltered valley in all its
glory. There it lay, the fairy valley, uninhabited and
neglected, but not for long.

' "Although tourists were scarce in those days, and
their visits like those of angels were few and far between, an Englishman saw this valley and became so
charmed with it that he built a neat slated cottage there.
This turned out to be fortunate for the natives. His
name was Daniel Bowden Smith, a retired Governor of
Bengal, who was passionately fond of fishing, and here
he could enjoy it to his heart's content, for the lake at
the foot of the valley abounded with salmon. He was
also fond of sea-fishing, and he rented and fitted out
for himself another neat cottage on Meenish Island,
adjacent to Carna, where he became acquainted with
the parish priest. The acquaintance ripened into friend-
ship, and they became inseparable friends.

' "Mr. Smith spent his time pleasantly going up and
down between his two cottages which lay nine miles
apart. Then the great famine of 1846 set in, and the
peasantry all around began to starve for they dwelt far
away from the great towns and cities. Then Daniel
Bowden Smith, the Englishman, began to stir himself.
He ordered boilers from Dublin, each capable of holding
forty gallons of water, and set them up. Then he employed men and women to attend to them, boiling

stirabout to feed the starving peasantry, and he hired a
family named Kelly to serve it out. Day and night, the
boiling was kept going for two and a half years, and
Daniel Bowden Smith saved thousands from death.

' "In 1849, some Connemara boatmen took down the
cholera from Galway where it was raging at that time.
Mr. Smith took the plague on Meenish Island and died
there. The man from whom he rented the cottage, and
who was always his skipper, stuck to him during his
illness, coffined and buried him in the Protestant cemetery in Roundstone, and the skipper escaped the plague
unscathed. Then the house in the valley became a ruin,
and some vandal took it away. The house should have
been preserved forever as an everlasting memorial of
one of the greatest Englishmen who ever figured in
Irish history. Alas, nothing now remains of it but its
foundations, nor is there anyone alive today in Ireland
who remembers him save myself. Five years from the
time he died, his name was obliterated from the minds
and memories of the ungrateful people he rescued from
a horrid death.

' "When I was leaving the valley where Daniel
Bowden Smith once ministered to a starving people, I
heard a sound that shook the great hills, and which
echoed through the mountains until it died away like
distant thunder. Again it was repeated, and yet again.
It was the sound of some enormous trumpet, and then
I realized, God help me, that the last day, the crack of
doom, had come and I was called across the Jordan. I
stood there in a quandary and began to cogitate. I said
to myself, 'I don't see why I should undertake a journey
to Palestine when there seems to be no compulsion,
nor do I see any disturbance or upheaval of nature. In
all my life I have never been brought before a court of
justice for any criminal offence. Why now should I
voluntarily offer myself in order to undergo such an
ordeal before the Court of Heaven, and perhaps to be
convicted?' 'No,' I said, 'I won't go unless I am propelled
by some supernatural force.' So once more I turned my
face to the South and proceeded on my way.

' "When I mounted a hillock I beheld the sea with

the evening sunbeams dancing on the bright waters of Roundstone Bay, some nine miles distant, and my heart rejoiced and was as glad as that of Xenophon and his ten thousand Greeks when they first beheld the sun in their retreat from Persia, or as that of Pizzaro and his followers when they beheld the Pacific from the summit of the Rocky Mountains. The peninsula I had come to explore came in view with the dark blue Isles of Aran far away on the rim of the ocean. There it lay before me, this strange region with its innumerable lakes, its soft moors of vast extent in which rugged hills stood up like cocks of hay in vast meadows, all flanked towards the South by a great, long, brown mountain on whose summit there was discernible a lofty Martello tower.

' "As I approached the soft moor which separates the peninsula from the mainland, I was confronted by a dwarf, or rather a pigmy, the strangest looking mortal I have ever seen. He was about four feet high, and he wore a high Jerry felt hat; his double-breasted coat was of brown frieze, and the buttons on it were as large as a small saucer. The coat would fit Jack na Bauna on his largest day, and yet this wee man filled it, and it hung on him with grace and dignity.

' "His vest was of the same frieze material and double-breasted, and from it there dangled a closed jack-knife of at least three pounds in weight. His little breeches were of corduroy and his short legs were encased in a capital pair of brown, boxcloth leggings. Under his arm he carried a common tin bugle as large as any churn dish I ever saw. 'God save you, neighbour,' he said in Irish. 'You infernal little villain,' I said, 'was it you blew the three blasts?' 'Yes, astore, I blew three little shadeognes,' he said, 'in order to inform the people of the country and the adjacent islands that I have arrived among them.' 'Who or what are you?' I asked. 'Moorkuseen na Muck, from Bohermore in Galway, and I cut animals of all genders,' he said. I left him in disgust and turned away.

' "I crossed over the soft moor safely and reached a great mountain which is considered one of the wildest and most precipitous in Connacht, and as I entered a narrow glen at the foot of the mountain I saw an unexpected sight, a granite glacier which slanted down from a cliff near the summit. Since the time of creation, every winter the great boulders falling down from the cliff have polished this inclined path as smooth as a mirror. It is eternally wet, so that any living thing that attempts to pass across it is swept down and crushed against the great boulders at the bottom.

‘ "As I drew near this spot, I saw a dead man in the glen at the foot of the glacier. He lay on his stomach, and his eyebrows, lips and nose were worn away by the friction and speed of his descent, and the ribs of his left side were driven in by the force of the impact. Against a large boulder beside him lay a tailor's lap-board, and out of his coat pocket protruded a large, black bottle, corked but unbroken. Horrified, I fled away from the place, and hastened to seek a rude cabin where some kind peasant would offer me a tumbler of poteen to forget the memory of that swift, terrifying death. Such sights are graven in my memory as I recall that perilous journey through the wilds of Connemara." '

To the World's End

‘Well,’ said the old smuggler from Achill, ‘in conse-quence of all the old legends that Brian McNamara was relating, and all the wild scenery he was describing, my head was almost turned upside down, so I cried out to him. "Brian, dear, I must see some of these places before I leave dear old Ireland, for maybe I shall never return. Anyhow, I must surely see Lough Inagh, the Prince of Lugatheriv, his castle and his fair daughter."

‘ "You can see all these things," he replied, "but I fear you shall not see that lovely girl."

‘ "Why not, Brian?" I asked.

‘ "Because," said he, "for the last three years she keeps to the castle in such a way that it would fail Don

Quixote in his best days to be able to get a chance of kissing his hand to her."

'When the Rapparee ceased speaking, he drained his glass, so I said to him, "Brian, I will sail from here tomorrow, for this is a dangerous bay for a smuggling craft to be anchored in." "How is that?" he asked. "Because there is no way of leaving it save by the channel I entered," I replied. "By gad, you are right; isn't it strange I never thought of it?" he said. "Do leave then, George, and don't delay, for if a cutter came in you would be caught in a trap, but I regret that I cannot accompany you." "Why not?" I asked him. "What is there to hinder you?"

' "I must say farewell to a very dear friend before I leave Ireland," he answered. "And who is that?" "Well," he said, "I was never any good at prevarication, consequently I will answer you truthfully. I must say farewell to Nula O'Flaherty, the fair daughter of the Prince of Lugatheriv, before I leave Ireland, for we love each other very dearly. If it costs me my life, I shall do it.

' "For three long, weary years," continued the outlaw, "I have attended Mass each Sunday in the little chapel on the vast moor, in rain and in sunshine, in snow and in frost, in order just to see the back of her glorious regal head as she knelt in her pew before the altar, for it is seldom I beheld her beautiful face. Then I would leave the chapel and climb to my home among the great cliffs of Benlethry, quite contented and happy. Sometimes I cross the Killary and climb to the summit of the stupendous Mweelrea in order to have a fond look at my native barony, Clew Bay, and the blue hills of far distant Tyrawley, and then my mind is at ease for a little while. These are the safety valves which keep my heart from breaking," he said with a sigh.

' "Just a few days before I first met you," he said, "I set out in order to visit Colonel Firebal McNamara, who lives in Cratloe in the County of Clare, and he received me kindly, for he is a distant relative of mine. He offered to keep me for life, or at least until the present storm of hunting exiles and outlaws exhausts itself, but when I awoke on Saturday morning, I

thought of the fair girl who would kneel at the altar
rails in the little church. I thought of how she would
miss me the next day, and of how I would miss her,
so I sprang out of bed and set out for Ballyvaughan.
There I went on board a Connemara hooker that landed
me at Carna. From there I set out across the vast moors
and rugged hills towards Killary, a distance of thirty
miles. I did not taste any food until I went on board
the lugger, but I had my reward, for the next day I saw
her at Mass," he said with a smile. "If you permit me to
accompany you, I will remain another day," I said. "All
right, George," he replied.

'Next morning we set out early, heading South. The
summits of the great hills were hidden by a canopy of
clouds, white and transparent, which melted away before the face of the sun, and the bare, damp granite of
the mountains glittered like burnished silver. We soon
came in sight of beautiful Lake Inagh where on the
western bank there stood the dark castle of the redoub-
table Prince of Lugatheriv. When we drew near it, quite
unexpectedly we met the Prince himself descending the
mountain carrying a young red deer in his arms. We
exchanged salutations and he, with his wonted hospitality, invited us to partake of some refreshments,
although we were strangers.

'When we entered the ground floor of the castle, his
wife, whom we had seen at the station dinner at Roger
Coyne's house, recognized and welcomed us. She was
surrounded by at least half a dozen poor peasant girls,
busily engaged at household domestic occupations. Some
were carding and spinning wool of various dyes; some
were engaged at the laborious work of making a heavy
churning, while more sat at a stack in the corner engaged in the most laborious work of all, cleaning and
thickening a large web of frieze and flannel, a substitute
for a tuck mill. There they sat, kicking against one
another like fury.

'The Prince then led us by a stone stairs to a
chamber on the second storey which was, I am certain,
the grandest apartment in all Ireland. The walls were
upholstered with the skins of wild animals, and the floor

was carpeted in a similar manner. Four windows, facing
the four points of the heavens, were glazed not by glass
but by a substance made of boiled bull's horns, a
transparent substance which filled the room with a
brown, mellow light, giving it an Oriental appearance.
It was a chamber in which a Calypso or a Circe would
love to recline and display their immortal charms to
the enamoured gaze of Ulysses with, I fear, fatal results.
Just opposite the castle there stood in the lake a thickly
wooded island in which the fair daughter had a summer
house, or greenan, and the wild notes of her harp were
wafted towards us across the still waters. Alas ! that
was the last time her white hands would ever touch the
silver strings of that much-loved harp.

'We were pressed to take food, but we declined, so
our hostess brought forth a great tankard of punch, but
not of the ordinary kind. It consisted of boiled goats'
milk, mixed with double distilled poteen, sweetened
with honey, a beverage fit for the gods. The drinking
vessels were finely polished bulls' horns, embellished
with quaint, antique tracery, far more ancient than that
of the Book of Kells. When we had partaken freely of
this wonderful mixture, we departed.

'In crossing a deep ravine which ran down to the
lake, we beheld with much pleasure the fair girl coming
towards us with a great bouquet of white and yellow
water lilies on her arm, and she looked so fresh and
lovely that I thought she could not be a mortal being.
When she drew near, smiling as she advanced, she
placed the flowers on the grass, ran forward, and
clasped her arms around the outlaw's neck. She drew
down his head towards her and kissed him on the brow
and then on the lips, while I stood looking on in
bewilderment.

'Then she unclasped her arms and said, "My own
darling Brian, it is three long and weary years since I
kissed you last."

' "It seems to me almost a lifetime," he replied. "Nula,
my love, I have come to say goodbye for a little while,
as I wish to accompany George, the smuggler, on a
voyage to Spain."

' "If you did, I would surely die, for it is the consciousness of your being somewhere near me which has upheld and sustained me up to this moment. My health is undermined by mental worry and suspense, Brian," she said, while her lustrous eyes dilated, "you have startled and forewarned me, so from this night forward, I shall forsake home and parents and follow you to the world's end. And now," she cried, with a sob, "I swear here, at the foot of my ancestral mountain, that dead or alive, alive or dead, I will sail with you on board the lugger." Then she kissed him once more and took up her flowers.

'When she was some distance from where we stood looking after her, her strength seemed to fail her, and she fell forward on the heather. We hastened to her assistance, but all of our efforts to revive her proved fruitless; the young woman was dead, and her pure soul had fled to Heaven. There she lay in all her youth and beauty a lifeless corpse, and in his anguish and despair, Brian cried out, "O Lord, Thou hast destroyed the noblest work of Thy hand." Well might he have cried out in his bereavement:

> "Oh, ever thus from childhood's hour,
> I've seen my fondest hopes decay,
> I never loved a tree or flower,
> But was the first to fade away;
> I never nursed a gay gazelle,
> To glad me with its fond dark eye,
> But when it came to know me well,
> And love me, it was sure to die."

'Although the outlaw's heart was broken, he somehow pulled himself together, for he realized our dangerous position. He said, "Keep cool and collected, for if the girl's father thinks that we, or at least I, had any hand in bringing about the girl's death, our blood will soon stain the heather. Stand off on that hillock while I go to inform her parents." He went on to the castle and informed the parents that while we were going through the glen we found the young woman in a swoon or else dead, we could not say, because we were loath to touch her. Their astonishment and grief were something terrible to witness. On examination, the father pronounced her dead, so he took her in his arms and carried her to the castle, while the great hills reverberated with the cries and lamentations.

'The wake was truly a Celtic one, carried out in every detail according to the orthodox rules and customs of the country, and her funeral to Salruck was one of the largest ever seen wending its way to that wild, romantic spot. While they were opening the grave, I was much interested in looking at the Alpine scenery which is unsurpassed by any other in Ireland, so I quite forgot the outlaw. When the grave was closed, and all was over, the outlaw was gone, nor was there any trace of him, although I sought for him everywhere until the shades of evening were descending. It flashed into my mind that he must have cast himself into the little bay and put an end to his existence. More dead than alive, I wended my lonely way to the ship and went on board.

'When the crew were piped down for the night, I began to pace the deck in great mental agony about the fate of my unfortunate friend, whose forlorn condition was a pathetically sad one. It is a terribly weird thing to be anchored alone in the Killary at night time, for the narrow bay seems to contract itself while the great mountains which enclose it on all sides seem to draw near. Being much worried and sleepless, that night my mental faculties became somewhat confused. I imagined I was anchored on a lake at the bottom of some enormous volcano whose crater gaped three thousand feet above me, and to make my predicament even more impossible, there was no egress from this lake. I sat down by the rudder and began to wipe the perspiration from my throbbing brow. Suddenly there was a slight sound borne by the night air, and as I listened I heard it again.

'It was the sound of oars dipping in the water, followed by the familiar rattle of the rowlocks. The sound grew louder, and soon I saw a boat approaching. In the bow sat a man pulling vigorously on the oars, and on

the stern sheets there was a coffin; my hair stood on
end, for I imagined it was Charon ferrying some dead
monarch across the dark waters of the Styx. Falteringly
I cried out, "In the name of God, who are you?" The
response came back, "Brian, the Rapparee."

'With a vigorous back stroke, he ran his skiff beside
the lugger. "What is that on the stern sheet?" I asked.
"It is the coffin and the corpse of my wife," he responded, "for we were married three years ago in the
great cave of Benlethry by the Augustinian Friar, Father
Myles Prendergast, once of the Abbey of Murrisk. When
she came to thank me for saving her life, Nula insisted
that we should get married and await better times; so
we parted at the mouth of the cave. Nor had we an
opportunity of speaking again until the day she died."

'All this was surely a revelation to me. "What do you
intend doing now with the remains?" I asked. "I expect
you will take it on board for a few hours," he said.
"Why should we do that, Brian?" I asked. "On your way
tomorrow you could land us at High Island, midway
between Boffin and Slyne Head," he replied. "In that
island there are many hermits' cells. I shall bury her in
one of them, and I shall live and die there, for I killed
her, and I am determined to atone for it."

' "How will you be able to support yourself?" I
asked. "I have my gun," he answered. "The island
abounds in rabbits, wild geese, and all kinds of sea-fowl
which I shall shoot, for I never fired at any living thing
that I did not kill. From the rocks all kinds of fish can
be caught, and I am a capital deep sea fisherman. Sure,
if I do starve, I have none to mourn or regret me."

' "What do you intend doing with the corpse if I do
not take it on board?" I asked. "I will row down the
bay; then I will place the coffin on the gunwale and
lash myself to it with the mooring rope, and shove it
overboard so that we will sink together," he answered.

'I saw the man was mad, and would do just as he
said, so I took the coffin aboard and placed it in a
slanting position against a bulkhead in the hold of the
vessel. Then Brian took a marline spike and started
prising the lid off the coffin. He folded back the shroud,

and there she stood before us dressed in the same cream-coloured dress she wore on the night of the station dinner, nor was there any sign of decomposition about her lovely face.

'Brian sat down on a sea chest, nor could all my per-suasions induce him to leave off looking at her. Next morning I set sail, with the wind from the south-east. When I reached the open sea there was a great ground swell, and the waves were thundering against the wild headland of Renvyle. My heart sank within me, for well I knew I could not touch the High Island, which was almost inaccessible even in the finest weather, and yet I longed to be rid of the mad outlaw and his grim burden. We had Boffin on our lee, and the white spray rose and raved and dashed against the ruined fortress on its most southerly point, once the stronghold of the Duke of Lorainne; on those ramparts I had often stood and pondered in former days.

'When we came in sight of High Island with its great crag standing on the brow of its western cliff, the most picturesque object is this, I thought, that the eye looks upon on the road leading to Cleggan from Claddaghduff. There it stands, its spires and pinnacles silhouetted against the dark western horizon like the towers and steeples of the Kremlin in Moscow. When we drew closer, the island was enshrouded in fog, and the great waves foamed and roared all around it. I went below and told the outlaw there was no hope of landing there.

' "Well," he said, "try to land me in St. MacDara's, or on one of the Brannock islands west of Aran.' When I rounded Slyne Head I had to take in sail, as from this point we encountered a head wind, for the coast line runs from here due East to Galway, some sixty miles distant. When I hove to in order to take in sail, a round hill of sea arose beneath us, raising us on its crest some fifty feet; then it fell away so suddenly that the craft plunged helplessly down with a crash, and I thought my day had come. Luckily, we had her under way before we reached another such wave, so she lay off towards the southwest on the tack out to sea.

'I went below then to see how it fared with the

Rapparee. The coffin lay flat on the sheeting, and I was amazed to see the Rapparee on his knees with the corpse in a sitting position and his arm around her. "Oh, great Lord," I said, "Brian, why have you disturbed the dead?" "Quick," he shouted, "get me some brandy, for she is coming to life!"

'When I returned with the brandy, she was yawning feebly, so when she opened her mouth I administered about a quarter glass carefully. She gave a stronger yawn, and I found myself doing the same. Then her body shook; her eyelids began to quiver, and soon she opened those magnificent eyes, looked around her, and said, "In the name of God, where am I?"

' "You are on board the lugger and in the arms of your husband," answered the outlaw. She was quite conscious now, and said jestingly, "Now didn't I swear I would sail with you on the lugger." We took her to the cabin where she partook of some refreshment.

' "Cheer up, Nula," I said, "for in two or three hours I will land you in Cloonisle at the head of Roundstone Bay, within some four miles of your father's castle." She shook her head and replied, "Never will I return there. This is the third time Brian has saved my life, so we will go with you to Spain, and we may find some means of going from there to Jamaica."

'At that time there was no emigration from the West to the States, so any person who emigrated went to Jamaica, because some generations before many thousands of the peasantry of the West were transported to Jamaica by the inhuman Cromwell, and those who left Ireland later for Jamaica thought they would meet some of the descendants of their relatives on that island, but as far as tradition goes, I never heard that they did meet any of them. When the Rapparee and his wife refused to return to the mainland, I lay off towards the Blaskets. When we were windward off the Skiards, a great brig bore down towards us, outward bound from Galway. I hove to and hailed her, for I had known the owner for many years. There were at this time three brothers who were sea captains in Galway whose name was Yorke. Each had a ship, and each acted as captain or skipper, and they generally traded with Jamaica.

'The brig swung around and shook out the wind and I boarded her, but I was greatly disappointed to find it was not Captain Yorke who was in charge of her, but a young Galway man named Hart, whom I also knew. He informed me that Captain Yorke was suddenly taken ill, and as the ship was chartered to sail the next morning, Yorke employed Hart to run this trip for him. I told Hart the sad story of the Rapparee and his fair young bride. "If they are determined to go to Jamaica," he said, "I will take them there with pleasure."

'I returned to the lugger and told the couple that Captain Hart was willing to take them to Jamaica, and they were overjoyed. I offered the Rapparee twenty pounds. "Take it," I said, "and whenever you feel able to pay me back, you can return it to me." "Oh, no," he answered. "When I fled to Connemara, my friends sold whatever means I possessed and sent the money to me; so I don't need it, but I thank you all the same." Then they went on board; the great ship bore around and her sails filled out before the wind, and she bore off towards the land of the setting sun, while I lay off towards the Blaskets.

'But,' said the old smuggler, 'from that day to this I never got tale or tidings of Brian McNamara or his fair young wife, Nula O'Flaherty. Years later I met a Captain Stone, a Galway man, in Flushing, and I asked him had he been to Jamaica since I last saw him. "Often," he said. I asked him did he ever meet or hear anything about the Rapparee. "No," he said, "how could I when I never knew him at all?"

' "However," he continued, "I can tell you about Johnny Hart and what he did to Captain Yorke's ship. When Hart took in a cargo of wine, rum, brandy and tobacco, he set sail from Jamaica, but not for Ireland. Instead, he bore off for Cape Horn, which he successfully rounded; then he ran down the Pacific, and never lowered a sail until he dried Captain Yorke's ship at high water mark on the strand of the bay of San Francisco, where now stands the great city.

' "He took out her masts and upset her; then he cut

doors and windows in her sides and turned her into a grog ship where he began selling their beloved fire water to the red men and the settlers. Later on, gold was discovered by a settler who was making a millrace, and who instead found gold within four inches of the surface. The clay which the first invaders put to back up the rude bridges was found to be all gold, so that in fact millions of settlers soon gathered there. Gold was so plentiful that if a person brought a gallon of milk to the miners he would get the gallon full of gold dust in exchange for it.

' "The wealthy miners soon began to build houses around the drinking saloon, the ship. In course of time, a great city sprang up around her, and this accounts for how low down near the water's edge the great city stands, for it is only from twelve to eighteen feet above sea level. And the strangest thing of all is that in the city, which was founded of robbing Captain Yorke of his ship, his grandson, Dr. Yorke, is now Vicar General. Surely the ways of Providence are strange and inscrutable."

'I agreed with him on that,' said the old smuggler with a wistful smile. 'But I would give the world and all to know what ever happened to the last Rapparee of the West, the brave Brian McNamara, and his lovely bride, Nula O'Flaherty, the only daughter of the Prince of Lugatheriv.'

The Man-Hunt

On my first visit to the peninsula where Carna is located, I encountered many dangers as I made my way through the wild, mountainous but always beautiful region. One evening, as the shades of night were closing around me, I reached a great rugged hill all strewn with whinstone boulders. A narrow strip of moor ran along its base, which was bounded by a long, narrow lake.

When I had traversed about half the length of the lake, I saw in the twilight some white object under a small hillock at the end of the lake.

I thought it was a sheep, as it seemed to be stirring, but when I drew near, it arose with a bound and stood before me on the path. It had the shape or outline of a human being of enormous stature, and was enveloped in a winding sheet which was all stained in patches as if by the decomposition of the corpse in the coffin, and although I could not see its face or hands, which were concealed, it was hideous to look at, as it began to prance in a zig-zag manner across the path from one side to the other.

My heart seemed about to burst and a cold thrill ran down my spine before my courage returned. I walked up to the demon, grasped my stick and struck it a terrible blow with my left hand across the right cheek and ear, or where they ought to have been, and it fell like a log to the ground. The winding sheet fell off and I saw a spent man who was almost naked, and he was bleeding from the ear and nose. He wore no shirt, and his thin, much-worn bauneen was pinned around his emaciated body with a long nail.

He had no trousers on, only thin, ragged drawers, and his long, spent shins and feet were naked. I was going to hit him a second time and dash out his brains, but, as I looked at him with his eyes closed, his mouth wide open, and his pale, bleeding face, I held my hand, for I was sure I had him finished. I then crossed the remainder of the moor and reached a long hill, overgrown with furze; from the summit I beheld Carna, the capital of the peninsula, standing on a granite rock some two hundred feet above the soft moors which surround it. It stood there in the twilight, impregnable and inaccessible to all mankind save a native, for the swamps abounded with blind, mossy pools, all overgrown with bulrushes and wild sedge, so that one false step would precipitate the unwary into eternity, for he would sink, never more to rise to the surface.

I determined to lie down in one of the many shady bowers formed by the sweet-smelling whins and await the dawn when, perhaps, some native would be going towards the village, and I could follow him. Just then an accidental encounter relieved me of the dilemma, for some twenty milch cows came down the mountain and made for the village through the swamps. I followed them and soon found myself in Carna, the most famous village of the Barony of Ballynahinch. This celebrated village consisted of three houses, including the parish priest's residence, but yet it held sway evermore as being the richest village in far Connacht, a reputation which it keeps to this day.

Troubled in my mind about the man against whom I had delivered what must surely have been a death blow, I went straight to the parish priest's house. His Reverence was sitting in the kitchen, eating some stirabout. When he had carefully scanned my face and appearance, he said abruptly, 'Pray, who are you?' I said I came from West Mayo and told him of my travels. 'You have received some shock. What is it?' he asked. 'Father,' I said, 'I fear I have killed a man.' 'Oh, great Lord !' he exclaimed in astonishment. 'Why did you kill him?'

'He posed as a ghost, and thought to frighten and un-nerve me, and then I dare say he intended to thrash me, but I struck him, and when the blow fell I found this was a man, not a demon as I thought at first.'

'How did you come to know he was a mortal?' he asked. 'Because when he fell, his disguise dropped away, and he was bleeding from the ear and nose,' I answered.

'Where did this happen?' he inquired. 'At the foot of a vast low hill along whose eastern shore there lies a long narrow lake about two miles from here,' I said. When I mentioned the place, the priest's servant who was standing in the corner seemed much affrighted.

'Oh, yes,' answered the priest, 'I know it well. For years that lake has been haunted by a ghost, a giant who rises out of the lake and thrashes all who pass that way. Some years ago he thrashed my predecessor who was on a midnight call, and almost murdered him. In consequence of all this the lake is called Lough Boltha na Skalonga. Now I shall investigate this matter, and

find out who is the villain who for years has been
committing these outrages. Come along, boys,' he said
to his servant and to several other men who had come
in and were listening in the background.

'We wouldn't go with you to that lake tonight,' they
said, 'if you gave up Cishlan, Ballynahinch, and Dick
Martin's property.' 'Oh, yes, you shall go, for I will put
Dutch courage into you,' he said. 'Go and bring me a
jug of poteen,' he said to his servant. When the men
had quaffed the water of life they were then as brave
as British soldiers at the time of the South African war,
and they followed their master.

Nor were they long absent when they returned,
bringing the wounded giant with them, and they locked
him up in a barn. He belonged to a quiet family who
lived near Roundstone Bay. When he grew up, he went
beyond control and fled to the hills, his occupation
being milking the neighbours' cows, outraging the females who were caring for them, and acting the ghost
at night.

Next morning the priest sent for his friends who took
him away with them. Some three months afterwards he
broke loose again. He swam Ard Bay and reached
Meenish Island; he could swim like a fish, for the wild
waves beat and dashed against the gable of the rude
cabin in which he was born. When he reached the
island, he outraged a respectable girl, and she returned
home and told her relations and friends. She belonged
to the fiercest, the strongest and most relentless clan
in the peninsula. They rose to a man and followed the
villain, and then I saw a strange, terrible sight, a man-
hunt.

Surely it was the greatest marathon foot race of
traditional Irish history, for they covered a circle of at
least twenty-four miles through soft moors and rugged
hills, before the quarry was taken. He wasn't an idiot,
but a sane, wild, primitive man, who when he heard the
uproar of the wild swarm who were coming after him,
knew and realized that his last day on earth had come.
He knew that before night his eyes would close here on
earth, and would open in the Great Beyond. He knew

that if he jumped into the Crater of Vesuvius, this clan would jump in after him.

It was a race for life. The fleeing man had scarcely any clothes, but he was inured to hardship. He had no spare flesh on his bones, but he was determined to give a good account of himself. When the pursuers drew near, he cast himself into the bay which separates the island from the mainland, and when he reached it he shook himself like a spaniel and bounded towards the distant hills with the spring of a reindeer.

He bounded off through Rusheenacolla, Crumpaun, Carna, on through Lettercashel, and the romantic Letterpibram; he ran through Glinan, Shanock, Doonal, and scudded on along the shore of the placid, unfrequented Lough-a-wee, and the narrow, silent vale of Cowlaun, but still his infuriated pursuers were yelling at his heels. Then he turned to the East along the northern base of the precipitous Cnueg Mourdaun. When he reached the sequestered village of Derinish he wheeled towards the South along the western shore of the picturesque bay of Kilkieran, but still the relentless, swarthy islanders were on his track.

Then he ran through the great moor towards the village of Loughconeera, and dashed in and swam a salt water creek. And well he might, for certain death was just behind him. Then he ran through the villages of Kylesala, Crearagh More, and Rossdoogan, and through the neat, well-sheltered village of Kilkicran, but yet his terrible foes were roaring behind him as he fled. He went through Bouraghard and Ardmore, Calageenish and Rusheenacouagh, and those who were watching on the hill of Carna sent up a great shout when they saw him coming at Sheedowagh.

On he came, head in air, springing like a wild deer, but when he reached the creek and the island strand, some of the girl's friends captured him, nor did they ill-treat him. When the other pursuers arrived, or at least some of them, for many lay helpless and exhausted on the moors, they bound him with ropes. Then they put him on board a hooker and bore him off towards Cortag-a-Meela, which stands out in the sea of Moyle,

some twenty miles from any land, a rock which so
often sheltered the white swans, the children of Lir,
during their cruel enchantment.

They tied a chain around the man's body and attached
to the chain the great mooring stone of a herring net,
and they sank him in a hundred fathoms of water, nor
was there ever a question about this action any more
than if it were a dog to whom this was done. Some
weeks later, a young woman was missing, and could
not be found, although her friends searched and sought
for her everywhere. It caused a sensation for a time,
but the incident was soon forgotten, for every day had
its own outrages and sensations in that lawless country.

This girl had given birth to an illegitimate child by a
man named Cosgrave, but he seemed more troubled
than any of her relations by her disappearance. There
was some talk about the ghost-man having freed himself
from his chain, abducting and running away with the
girl, but most people thought this impossible.

Six months later, the girl's decomposed remains
floated ashore at the very door of her father's rude
dwelling, and her hands had been severed from the
wrists by some sharp instrument. Nine of the Cosgrave
clan were arrested on suspicion, and one of them became an informer. It developed that Cosgrave had sent
word to the unfortunate, unsuspecting girl to meet him
at a certain creek, where they would take a boat at
night in order to proceed to Roundstone to be married.

The girl readily agreed and went with the Cosgraves
in the boat. When midway between Moyrus and Roundstone, they threw her overboard. When she rose to the
surface, she caught hold of the gunwale of the boat
with both hands, which one of the villains cut off with
a hatchet. Then they tied her with the mooring rope
which was attached to a grapnel and sank her to the
bottom of the bay, and yet, strange to say, her remains
floated ashore. The chief culprit, Cosgrave, died in
prison; the informer was set free, and the remaining
seven scoundrels were transported for twenty years to
Van Diemen's Land.

The Secret Society of the Terryalts

At one time, many years ago, the peninsula near Roundstone was infested and overrun by the Terryalts. They
were a secret society like Whiteboys or Ribbon men,
introduced to Connemara, or at least this portion of it,
by refugees from Clare. They posed as patriots in
Munster, while here their patriotism consisted in going
about in broad daylight robbing and plundering the
wealthy peasantry, and a vast number of the natives
joined them. They attacked the homes of the well-off
people, taking away money, bacon, crocks of butter
and kegs of poteen.

On a certain day they surrounded the house of a very
wealthy man named Green. He was a boat builder who
had five fully-grown sons, all boat builders. The houses
in those days had no windows, so Green and his five
sons stood in the doorway, each armed with an adze.
When the Terryalts thought to rush the door, which
Green had thrown open, the Greens attacked them with
their adzes. Some lost a hand, some a cheek, some a
nose or an ear, besides various other wounds. The
Terrys, as they were called, fled dismayed, carrying
their wounded with them.

When the peasantry saw how ably Green repelled
them, each family began to arm themselves, and the
robbing activities of the Terryalts were ended forever.
Then their captain, a black-haired, swarthy man of
enormous stature, went privately to Tom Martin of
Ballynahinch, and became an informer. He gave the
names of eighty of his accomplices, whose names were
sent off to Dublin Castle. They were all natives who
thought the captain was their friend.

There was consternation in the peninsula. The spy
thought his accomplices knew nothing about it, but in
this the villain was mistaken. The Terryalts assembled in
a graveyard and cast lots who would kill the spy, and of
course someone drew the fatal lot. There was to be a
fair held in Roundstone in a day or two, on June 29.
The accomplices were to begin a mock battle among

themselves, for they well knew the spy would interfere
to make peace, and in the melee they intended to kill
him.

Clever as the informer was, he was ignorant of all
this, while all the peasantry of the region knew his last
day was drawing near, for in every family there was a
Terryalt. The long expected day arrived, and there was
a vast gathering of the wildest men in Ireland in Roundstone on that day.

The battle began, amidst terrific noise and uproar.
The spy rushed in, and in a moment he was hit with a
long splinter of granite, which buried itself behind his
ear, sinking far into his head. He fell down with a
crash, stark dead, and in a twinkling there was not a
trace of the crowd, nor was an inquiry ever made about
the slaying.

The body lay on the street in Roundstone all that long
summer's day, and when I looked at the dead villain
with the long splinter driven deep into his brain, I
thought of the other villain Connor McNessa, lying with
the brain ball of his foe buried deep in his head.

The Village of Carna

When I first visited Carna in Connemara, it was known
as the richest village in that region, although there were
only three houses there at the time. It was evermore the
mistress of the Barony of Ballynahinch, and in all prob-
ability it will remain so, for its present citizens are
among the wealthiest in the province. Thank God and
Nature, our granite quarries are supposed to be the
finest in Europe, and our mines and other minerals are
inexhaustible. The two lay inhabitants who dwelt there
when I arrived were very rich, indeed, one of them exceedingly so.

He had one hundred and one milch cows, eighty-two
breed mares, and I well recollect that one May morning
twenty-six of these mares had twenty-six filly foals. He

had 550 heifers, for in that country they never reared a bullock until after the Crimean war. He had a couple of thousand sheep, and two thousand yellow, gold sovereigns sewed carefully away in his feather bed. Now, wasn't he a wealthy man?

I have seen some strange things in my time, but the strangest thing I have ever seen was this man twenty years afterwards without a cow, calf, sheep, or horse, nor a four-footed animal, nor a brass farthing of money. The only cause the natives would or could assign for his poverty was that he added length to his dwelling-house towards the West. 'How on earth could that bring about his poverty?' I said to a native. 'Oh, sure, there is an Irish proverb which says, "He is stronger than God who puts length out of his house towards the West".'

The other citizen was reputed to be worth two thousand pounds. He was married, but had no family, and his queen was supposed by the natives to be the heaviest woman on earth, for she was twenty-seven stone weight. He kept a public house, where he sold the wildest and strongest fire-water on earth, and yet the natives drank it like nectar. He often went across the great mountains and vast moors to Galway, some fifty miles distant, in order to buy this terrible stuff, and also to buy Clough Gorm or blue stain to put on it, for if it didn't scald the necks out of them the natives wouldn't be bothered with it.

The night before starting for Galway he always boiled a skillet of potatoes, which he packed a pair of socks with. He then pinned the mouths of the baileens together and slung them across his shoulder, and these cold, boiled potatoes, without any relish, was his lunch on his journey. When returning, he always slept in a cave formed by three enormous, granite rocks on the verge of a vast moor midway between Carna and Recess.

This unfortunate man also began to build a room towards the West. When it was side wall high, both he and his wife fell sick and were given over as practically dead. In great haste, then, they sent a trusty friend to old Mother Clifden, the witch. 'The crime is a heinous

one,' she said, 'for he blocked the path where the fairies
sleep at night, and where they pass frequently. I see
blood on one of the cornerstones; the woman will recover, but the husband must perish for his crime is
beyond forgiveness.'

The woman recovered; then she took possession of
the sick man's money and sold all his stock. She
knocked down the new wall, and she very quietly
starved the husband in the corner where he lay. He
died, alas, without a four-footed beast, nor a farthing
of money. The widow married a policeman, and whatever she did to the first husband, the second one gave
her twice as much, and thereby hangs another tale.
Another man arose phoenix-like out of the ashes of
these two men, and like them he was wealthy, aspiring
and impudent. But, like them, he finished off his old
age without a beast or a foot of land. Surely, there must
be some terrible malediction hanging over that fatal
stock.

The inhabitants of the peninsula were, I am certain,
the wealthiest peasantry in Connacht, as far as stocks
and boats went. Each family had at least twenty cows,
ten or fifteen brood mares, and from three to five score
heifers, with sheep in abundance, and the dowry of
each peasant girl when getting married was twenty-one
cows and a bull.

Each family owned a hooker, some two, while others
had four of them, and thirteen or fourteen smaller ones
for various purposes. In the spring, each family sent at
least forty hooker loads of black seaweed to Ballyvaughan, Kinvara, and Cranmore, and they generally
sold at three pounds per load. In May and June each
family sent at least forty hooker loads of turf to the
Isles of Aran and to the towns which I have named;
they got fifty shillings per load for the turf.

The month of July they spent fishing gunnard, of
which they caught and sold a great quantity. In August
they went out of sight of land in search of the basking
sunfish, those lazy monsters of the deep. During the
season, each boat would harpoon from five to seven of
these monsters, and the liver of each fish was worth

thirty-five pounds. The harpoons of these stalwart, intrepid men are to be seen to this day behind the rafters
in the homes of their diminutive descendants. In winter
they made enormous sums on the herring fishing, for
at times a hooker load was worth as much as sixty
pounds. Alas ! artificial manure, coal, and railways have
played out all these industries. In 1845 there were five
hundred and fifty hookers; in the present year (1911)
there were only five hookers in all of this once wealthy
peninsula.

There was no kind of pasture anywhere, for the soft
fens and moors ran down to the water's edge, so the
peasants kept their cattle on the numerous, adjacent hills
all the year round, but in winter they hand-fed the
cows twice a day. It was a grand, interesting sight to
see those cows when the usual meal hour drew near.
There they would stand on the terraces and plateaus
perched high, gazing southwards towards the island and
the villages along the shore, waiting expectantly for
their owners, gazing as Jacob of old gazed wistfully
towards Egypt awaiting the return of his sons with the
long-expected, much-needed corn.

When the owners of the cows drew near, the animals
would rush headlong down the precipitous declivity,
lowing with joy, like a sallying party from an almost
famished, beleagured city hastening to meet a convoy of
friends laden with food for their relief. And when I saw
this wild, headlong rush, it often brought to my memory
that incident mentioned in Roman history, how when
the greatest general of antiquity, Hannibal, was hemmed
in by his enemies amid the ravines of the Italian mountains, he let down droves of wild oxen on Fabius and
his Roman legions.

Now when I reached this far-famed village of Carna
where, all unknown to me at that time, I was to marry,
settle, rear my family, and eventually to have my bones
interred, I inquired for and had pointed out to me the
parish priest's house, which was a long, one-storey
thatched cottage with three chimneys. I understood he
was a West Mayo man who was far-famed for his
hospitality towards strangers. When I entered, His

Reverence was seated in the kitchen talking to four or
five men of various ages who seemed to be servants. He
arose and began to scrutinize me very critically, and I
also began to take his measure, for I had often heard of
him, but had never before seen him.

He was middle-sized and middle-aged, with straight
black hair tinged with grey, and he was just beginning
to develop the worst load a man ever carried, namely, a
paunch. His nose was long and inclined to turn up, and
his brown eyes were large and lustrous. Trousers
weren't worn then by clergymen, so his lower limbs
were encased in knee-breeches and black broadcloth
leggings. This was the priest who when a young man
took the great ride from Tully to Leenane on Maura-
nee-Ortha, and who was the best-known and most
popular priest who ever figured in the Barony of Ballynahinch since the days of St. Mac Dara, and the most
hospitable, considering the smallness of his revenues
and resources. Although the savage peasantry whose
spiritual wants he attended to were surely the wealthiest
in Connacht, they scarcely gave him anything.

His Christmas collection never exceeded twenty-three
pounds, while his Easter one never exceeded seventeen
pounds, and sometimes fell to thirteen pounds.

> 'A man he was to all the country dear,
> And passing rich on forty pounds a year.'

Now this is one of the poorest parishes in Connacht,
and yet the Christmas collection is generally over one
hundred pounds, as is the Easter one. This may seem
curious, but it is easily accounted for, because the
people in the days when this was a wild region didn't
trouble themselves about religious matters until the
hour of death, but then, believe me, lukewarm as they
had been all their lives, there was a great parade of
messengers hastening across the soft moors and rugged
hills, calling for the Soggarth to hurry or you won't
catch him alive, Father, for the sick person wanted to
make a clean breast of it before he crossed the Jordan.

In fact, the priest would have starved among these

wealthy savages were it not that he owned a mountain farm of about four hundred acres, about sixty acres of which were arable, on which he reared ten or twelve cows, ten or twelve brood mares, about thirty heifers, and a hundred sheep. He also had a large tillage and pigs and poultry. Consequently, he was quite independent of them, and he needed to be.

When he began the confession stations, his servant took the vestment box on his back, and they set out across the great moors and steep hills to the most easterly village in the parish, a distance of twelve miles, for there were no roads in any portion of that wild peninsula. There he slept that night in one of the dark, rude cabins, and so on from village to village during the week, nor did he see his own house again until Saturday night. After three months of this kind of work, he had to do the same in the numerous islands off the wild shore. Imagine getting a midnight call to one of those far-away villages, or one of the storm-beaten islands, but yet it had to be done, for he had no curate until he got prematurely old and feeble.

The priest's house was like a home for the aged poor and the wandering outcast, for his door lay wide open to all in need.

> 'His house was known to all the vagrant train;
> He chid their wanderings, but relieved their pain.
> The long-remembered beggar was his guest,
> Whose beard descending, swept his aged breast.
> The ruined spendthrift, now no longer proud,
> Claimed kindred there, and had his claim allowed,
> The broken soldier, kindly bade to stay,
> Sat by the fire and talked the night away,
> Wept o'er his wounds or tales of sorrow done,
> Shouldered his crutch and showed how fields were
> won.'

Not many weeks ago, a distinguished priest was telling me that he was often called to attend a very respectable old woman who lived some four miles from Carna, and whenever he would arrive at her home, the

first question she would ask him was, 'How is the Ahir
Emon?' She forgot all the good priests who have succeeded him, but she never forgot the old friend who is
sleeping the sleep of the just in his neglected grave
since the tenth of June, 1859, that is, something over
half a century.

This was the grand and great Parish Priest of Carna,
that Father O'Malley who was the son of Paddy O'Malley of Shraugh, near Louisburgh in County Mayo, the
last packman of the West.